JUNE FOSTER

Thank you,
Cheryl

The Hidden Legacy

June Foster

Copyright © 2025 by June Foster
Published by Forget Me Not Romances

This book is a work of fiction. Names, characters, places, and incidents are the product of the author's imagination and are used fictitiously. Any resemblance to actual events, locales, or persons, living or dead, is coincidental.

All rights reserved including the right to reproduce this book or portions thereof in any form whatsoever – except short passages for reviews – without express permission.

All scripture is from the New International Version.

ISBN-13:978-1-968792-04-6

"Whoever welcomes one of these little children in my name welcomes me."

Chapter One

Austin Ford frowned as he reached for the old rag hanging on the hook near Jack's stall. "Hey, buddy, let me help you with that runny nose." He swiped the huge horse's muzzle and tossed the cloth into the bin with the other dirty ones.

For the fourth day now, Jack had hacked a harsh, dry cough. The animal likely had a cold, or perhaps even the flu.

Austin glanced at the feed trough still filled with the oats he'd given Jack last night. "What happened to your appetite?" He stroked Jack's mane and whispered, as if the poor animal was on its deathbed. "The vet will be here any moment. She'll know how we can get you well."

Dr. Lawson—the new vet in their small town of Oakville, Texas—how could he not choose her over the elderly doc who prepared to retire? After all, Chet recommended her, and if Dad's previous ranch hand endorsed her, she was fine by Austin.

Austin paced the space around Jack's pen. Dr. Lawson couldn't come any too soon.

Jack coughed again and took a raspy breath. Austin had made a wise move—isolating him in the unused section of the horse barn.

As if Jack needed a detailed explanation, Austin peered into the horse's eyes. "You've got the stall all to yourself. I don't want any of the other animals near you since what you have is probably contagious." Austin refilled Jack's water bucket and set it in his stall. "Hey, buddy. You're my favorite horse, you know. I want to see you get well." He chuckled. Jack probably didn't understand a word he said.

Twenty minutes later, the sound of a motor from the main highway informed him the vet had arrived. *Thank You, Lord. She's here.*

Austin stepped out of the horse barn and waved at the approaching van.

The vet parked her vehicle in front and got out. She marched toward him, her cowgirl boots leaving footprints in the reddish-brown soil. With her tight jeans and ponytail, she looked as if she should be working on a ranch instead of running a veterinarian's office.

How could that petite woman manage to treat a large horse like Jack without help? She couldn't have been more than five foot two. Dark brown almond eyes hinted of an Asian heritage.

Austin took a couple of steps toward her. "Thanks for coming. Jack's in here."

She held out her hand. "I'm Dr. Willow Lawson. Nice to—" Willow's eyes met his, and she stared for a moment. Then she gripped her throat and gasped. "No, it can't be …" She screamed and gasped again. "You're dead." A few seconds later, she slipped to the ground, falling onto a mound of soft dirt.

"Dr. Lawson." Austin dropped to his knees and cradled the woman's head and slim shoulders in his arms. "Doctor, are you okay? What happened?" He brushed a twig from her long, straight hair.

The doctor's bag lay a few feet from her. She moaned, and her long lashes fluttered.

What should he do? Perhaps take her up to the house and ask his mother to help? He slid one arm under her shoulders and the other under her knees. She was no heavier than one of the young lambs from last year's flock.

Near the front porch, the doctor stirred in his arms and opened her eyes. Again, she screamed. "Put me down."

The door opened, and Mom raced toward them. "Austin, what's going on?"

The vet, terror in her eyes, backed away from Austin and turned to Mom. "Please, I need your help."

"Yes, of course." Mom gently grasped Willow's

arm. "I'm Diane Ford. Please come in, and I'll fix you a cup of chamomile tea."

She clutched Mom's hand and stared at Austin again. "Who—who is that man?"

With a slight smile and a bit of a chuckle, Mom led the doctor into the house. "He's my son, Austin Ford. I assure you, Austin loves the Lord and would never harm you. He's my youngest at home now and has always respected women." She glanced over her shoulder as she led Dr. Lawson into the front room. "Sit here on the couch."

Dr. Lawson took another look at Austin and shook her head. "No, please don't leave me alone with him."

"Look." Mom pointed to the kitchen. "You can see me from where you're sitting." She peered at Austin and shook her head. "I have a kettle of hot water on the stove now. I'll be back with your tea in moments."

A flush heated Austin's face as he backed away and took a seat across the room. "Look, Doctor, I'm not sure who you think I am, but I guarantee I only called you to take a look at my horse, Jack. I'm afraid that if he doesn't get attention soon, he may be headed for trouble."

Hands shaking, the doctor clasped her throat again. "I—I'm sorry. I'm anxious to take a look at Jack and want to help him. It's just that … that you look exactly like … "

Austin scratched the side of his head. "I have

never met you in my life. I am not whoever you think I am."

Mom brought a cup of steaming tea and set it on the coffee table in front of the vet. "Here you go, dear. Drink a sip or two, and you'll feel better." Mom dropped down next to her on the couch.

The doctor sat up straight, grasped the handle of the cup, and sipped. She gave Austin one more quick glance.

Curiosity came close to overcoming him. He cleared his throat. "If I might ask, who do you believe I look like?"

"The exact image of—" She shifted on the couch and took another sip. "No, you'd think I've lost my mind." She glanced at Mom. "Thanks so much for the tea. I'm better now." She stood. "I can't allow Jack to suffer anymore. Let me see what I can do for him."

It's about time. Austin rose from his seat and held the door for her. "Jack is in his stall." This time, he prayed she wouldn't pass out when she arrived at the horse barn.

~

Willow glanced over her shoulder. She resisted the urge to panic once again as she walked with the rancher to the horse barn. How could any man look so much like—? No, she couldn't abide the thought. Whatever the answer to her question might be, Austin

Ford wasn't it. Her face warmed. The poor guy must've thought her an idiot. At the door, she paused and turned to him. "I'm sorry for my reaction a while ago. I'm sure you're a perfectly nice guy. I suppose I had a flashback to another time in my life."

Austin raised his hands, palms toward her. "Hey, no problem. I didn't know I was that scary looking, anyway."

She gave a laugh, one which helped release the tension in her neck. Her cheeks warmed again. She had to admit, this guy wasn't scary at all. He was a full-fledged cowboy in his tan Stetson and brown western-style shirt. In fact, he was one of the best-looking guys she'd seen since ... No, she couldn't go there.

Still, confusion threatened. How could anyone look exactly like Jesse and not be him? "Not at all. You didn't scare me." But now she needed to bring her attention to the sick horse. She picked up her bag she'd dropped in front of the horse barn and walked toward the stall where a reddish-brown stallion gave a deep dry cough. He stood listless as if he had no energy, and his nose ran with an obvious nasal discharge.

"This is Jack." Austin ran his hand alongside of the horse's head. "I'm afraid he isn't feeling well. He drank his water, but his food is still in the trough."

"Hey, Jack. You're not doing so good. Well, don't worry. We'll have you fixed up soon." She turned to Austin. "I need to get his temperature and take a nasal sample, but I suspect equine influenza." She pulled a pair of plastic gloves from her bag and tugged them on her hands. Then she listened to Jack's chest. "His breathing is labored." She inserted a thermometer, glanced at her watch for a minute, and pulled the instrument out. "Just as I thought. Jack has a fever. How long have you noticed his symptoms?"

Concern filled Austin's eyes. "A few days, I'm afraid."

"Hey, don't worry. We'll have him feeling better soon." She retrieved two swabs from her bag and ran them around Jack's nostrils. "Poor guy, he's feeling so bad, he didn't put up a fuss when I collected his nasal fluid." She placed the swabs in the sterile containers to send off to the lab. "I should have the results in a couple of days. In the meantime, I want you to give him these anti-inflammatory pills which will help with the pain and reduce the fever." She passed him the bottle of medication.

The rancher's green eyes with flakes of gold, so like Jesse's, twinkled in the low light of the barn. Was he trying to figure out what kind of woman would faint the first time she saw him? "Is there anything else I should do?"

"Yes, isolate him from your other horses. Allow him to rest at least two weeks. I'll know more when I get the results."

Discovering how Jack got sick would help. "Was Jack exposed to another horse who might've had an illness?"

Austin glanced at the vinyl-faced insulation of the ceiling. "Hmm. Oh, yes. My neighbor's horse. Last week, I worked Jack in the north pasture after dinner. I'd checked the fence line that day to see if any section needed repair. I still lacked about fifty yards." Austin caught her gaze and looked away again. "Mr. Whitlock who owns the ranch to the east rode up on one of his horses."

"Is that when you think Jack may have caught the flu?"

"Could be. Mr. Whitlock's horse came fairly close to my animal. He asked if I'd been working after dark lately. After I said no, he told me he'd seen flashing lights toward our north pasture a couple of nights ago. We rode over to the area. The oddest thing. There were holes in the ground as if someone had been digging."

Willow scratched her head. "It could've been an animal such as an armadillo or ground hog. But did you notice any signs his horse was infected?"

"No, I didn't see any symptoms."

"Unfortunately, some horses may not show outward signs of infection but could still spread the virus. Perhaps Jack caught the flu from your neighbor's horse." She gave Jack another pat on his head, picked up her equipment from the side table, and then chuckled. "About that neighbor, maybe instead of flashing lights, he saw an exploding meteor in the direction of your ranch."

He smiled. "Yep, maybe it was a meteor. Who knows?"

~

Austin watched Willow's van as she drove down the driveway and turned on the main road to town. He shook his head. He'd never met a woman quite like her before. Her reaction to him left him baffled. Screaming and fainting after she took one look at him. What was that all about? He shrugged and turned toward Jack's stall.

Poor guy. The flu. He knew the feeling as he'd wrestled with a bout of the stuff last winter. He glanced at the bottle of apple favored anti-inflammatory pills. Jack would likely take that without any argument. He held out one of the chewable pills, only a little larger than a human aspirin.

Jack sniffed the medication sitting on Austin's palm and took it with his lips, chewed, and swallowed. "Good boy. For that, you deserve a rub down. I'm sorry you got the flu from the neighbor's horse."

As if he understood, Jack bobbed his head up and down and then stood still for his brushing.

Austin ran the long, stiff bristles of the dandy brush over Jack's hair.

Jack gave a soft neigh as if saying thank you.

"You know, buddy, that lady vet screamed and fainted the minute she saw me. I don't get it."

Jack whipped his head around to Austin and then straightened again.

"She said I reminded her of someone. Whoever the guy was must've scared her." Austin took a long inhale. Having Jack to talk to wasn't a privilege he took for granted. "But if you want to know the truth, what bothers me the most is Mr. Whitlock from the ranch next to ours and his report that he'd seen lights out in the back pasture. On our property, too. I've got to get to the bottom of this."

After Jack's brushing, Austin filled his bucket with fresh water. "You still have your oats left from this morning. Try to eat something tonight."

Austin headed to the main house for dinner. Though he instructed Jack to eat his supper, after all that happened today, could Austin eat anything tonight?

Chapter Two

In Willow's clinic, the large border collie lay still on her examination table. "The plaster on Ranger's cast will take a few hours to dry." Willow ran her hand down the drowsy dog's fur and glanced up at her assistant. "Chet, please call Mr. Whitlock in. I need to give him a few instructions."

"Sure, Dr. Lawson." Chet took a few steps toward the door and then turned to her. "I'd like to thank you for giving me this chance to work for you. Maybe someday, I'll finally be a vet."

Willow smiled. No doubt Chet would achieve his goal given his determination to learn. He was a hard worker and from what she'd observed so far, truly had respect for an animal's good health. "I'm happy you're here."

Chet returned in moments, Mr. Whitlock behind him. The rancher took a guarded step toward his dog. "Will Ranger be okay?"

"Yes, sir. He's a young dog, and this break should heal quickly. However, he'll need to remain in the hospital overnight." Willow glanced at Chet. "Can you please prepare sixty caplets of Carprofen for Mr. Whitlock to take home." She stroked Ranger's fur again. "I recommend you keep Ranger in the barn or your house for at least six weeks to allow him time to rest. I'll make another appointment for you so I can check his progress, to see if he's fully healed and ready to begin his daily activities."

Mr. Whitlock stepped closer to the dog, his shoulders stiff, and his gaze locked on Ranger. He leaned toward the animal. "I have my suspicions about what happened. To the best of my knowledge, Ranger escaped the fence around my property and ran over to the Ford ranch." The rancher's voice caught. "Yesterday evening when I whistled for him, he didn't come. I feared the worst. Perhaps a coyote had gotten him. I took my ATV and found Ranger at my fence line with a broken leg." He scrubbed his hand over his chin. "I'm sure he fell into one of those blamed holes on Terrence Ford's ranch."

The Ford Ranch? Strange. She didn't want to start any feuds between neighbors, but Austin had told her Mr. Whitlock came to his ranch to ask about the disturbances in the north pasture. The way Austin described Mr. Whitlock's demeanor—tense, eyes narrowed—had sent a shiver down her spine. It was the kind of thing that could escalate quickly, especially when livestock were involved.

"Not only holes, but several weeks ago in the evening, I saw what looked like flashing lights from the Ford's north pasture. I didn't think too much about it, but later Austin was riding his horse by my fence. I hopped on my horse to ask if he'd been doing some night work. I told him I'd seen lights coming from over there. Together, we rode to where I'd seen the lights. There were at least ten holes—some deep, others about two feet."

Chet walked into the room. "Here's the medication you ordered."

"Good work, Chet." Willow unscrewed the top to check the pills and then handed the container to the rancher. "The instructions are on the front of the bottle. Come in tomorrow. Ranger will be ready to go home to his family. Around noon?"

Mr. Whitlock smiled as he turned to leave. "I appreciate it. I'll be here to get my dog. I think a lot of him, you know."

Willow stood straight and lifted her chin as a sense of pride washed through her. Not only did she treat animals, but she supported the folks who loved them. Her commitment to her profession was as natural for her as breathing.

Chet cautiously moved Ranger to the cage lined with a soft cotton towel. He refilled the water and the food bowls and then returned the X-ray machine to its place in the corner. "When did you first know you wanted to be a vet?"

"I suppose I knew from the time I was a little girl." Willow typed her notes into the computer on her desk explaining Ranger's procedure and prognosis. "When did you discover a love for animals?"

Chet looked at her over his shoulder, a wide grin on his lips and scrubbed the exam table with disinfectant. "When I started my job as a hand on the Ford ranch. Working around those animals, and all."

"Yes, your letter of recommendation from Mr. Ford speaks highly of you."

"Awe, thanks, doc." He continued to scrub, wiping the sink with a clean cloth and the sterilization solution. "Mr. and Mrs. Ford saved my life. They took me in and gave me a chance to work when I had nowhere else to turn. They even helped me connect with my little brother, Pete. As you know, me and Pete live with Mr. Ford's daughter, Erica, and her husband, Peyton, now. They own Horse Haven Boys' Ranch. And best of all, the Ford's took me to church and helped me learn about my Savior, Jesus."

Joy rushed through Willow's insides, and she lifted her hand in praise. He knew the Savior as she did. "You're becoming an experienced rancher, working at the Ford Ranch and then moving to Horse Haven."

"You bet. At the time, Peyton was one of the ranch hands, but he worked his way into Miss Erica's heart, and now, they're married. Got a baby, too."

Though she knew she shouldn't ask, she

couldn't resist. "What about Austin? Did you know him well when you lived on the ranch?"

"Austin and I always got along just fine. I think he's mostly responsible for the Ford ranch these days. Mr. Ford has slowed down a bit." Chet peered into Ranger's cage again. "You get well, now, boy."

Willow switched off her computer and straightened her desk. "It's almost time for you to go. See you tomorrow, and thank you for all your help."

"See you, doc. Have a good evening." Chet took off his lab apron and hung it on the hook near the sink.

Willow picked up the bottle of disinfectant and wiped down the pet scales, the IV pump, and the counter. Though Mr. Whitlock wasn't certain how Ranger broke his leg, another puzzle baffled her even more. Austin Ford.

How could the man look exactly like her late husband? Perhaps her imagination worked overtime.

~

Austin knocked on the door of the bunkhouse and pushed it open. "Hey, you coming up to dinner pretty soon, Mac? Betsy Whitlock's cooking."

Mac rose from his bed, setting his Bible on the night table. "So, are you hinting that her cooking is better than mine?"

Austin guffawed and slapped their ranch hand's shoulder. "Not at all, and especially when we get to sample your barbecue, friend. But if Betsy wasn't here to give you a break, you'd have to eat my cooking. You'd probably get a job at another ranch."

Mac chuckled. "You can count on that, Austin." He drew a comb through his hair. "But right now, I'm so hungry, I could probably eat something you made."

Austin gave Mac another shoulder punch. "Yeah, right." He lifted his palm to delay the ranch hand a moment. "I actually have a situation I need to talk to you about."

"What's up?" Mac raised his brow. "Couldn't be any worse than last year when Mr. Ford ran into those financial problems." He scratched his head.

Austin paced a few steps toward the center of the room and back again. "We're having a problem at the ranch. I'm not sure how this is going to work out, but I'd like for you to help Dad and me keep an eye on the back pasture, especially in the late evening or night."

Mac furrowed his brow as he rubbed the back of his neck. "What's going on?"

Austin cleared his throat, hoping that he could impress upon Mac the potential difficulties they could encounter. "Mr. Whitlock reported that he saw something shining in the north pasture a couple of weeks ago. He rode his horse to where he thought he'd seen the lights. He found a bunch of holes—as if someone had been digging. Willow Lawson, our new vet, says she believes the holes could have been made by animals. In any case, I'd like for you to keep your eyes open. Also, Mac, if you could let Pete know when he comes to work this weekend."

"Will do, boss." Mac gave a soft chuckle. "That Pete is the spitting image of his brother Chet and works just as hard. We're lucky to have him, even if he does go to school during the week, and we only get him on the weekends."

Mac walked beside Austin toward the ranch house. "Just wanted to say, I think you're doing a mighty fine job of taking more responsibility in running the ranch. I guess with Jace, Erica, and Peyton gone, it kind of leaves you in charge."

In charge? Austin ran the words around in his mind a couple of times. He'd have to get used to being the boss. "Thanks. Dad has backed off making some of his administrative decisions. It wouldn't surprise me if one of these days he announced he was retiring."

When they reached the front door to the house, Austin turned to the middle-aged ranch hand whom he'd known since he was a kid. "I have to admit, I'm feeling the weight of responsibility on my shoulders these days. More decisions have fallen to me plus a lot of the financial dealings. I'm grateful that the sheering is done for this year. Dad also said he wanted to handle the wool sales. That takes a little pressure off."

Mac held the door for Austin. "If you want to know my opinion, I believe he enjoys office work more than the rough and tumble ranch chores."

"Yep, and that's fine with me. He needs to slow down." Austin walked past Mac into the wide entryway.

Mac lifted his head high. "Look, buddy, God has this in His hands. All you have to do is ask Him to help."

Austin glanced away, not wanting Mac to see the emotion in his eyes. Mac had a close relationship with God. Though Austin loved the Lord, he needed to understand even more about his Savior.

~

After dinner, when Mac returned to the bunk house, Austin glanced from his mom to his dad across the table. "I need to talk a minute."

Mom leaned forward, her brows slightly raised, as if she couldn't wait to hear what he had to say.

Fine, he had no secrets from her.

Dad wiped his mouth with his napkin and turned to Austin. "Son, before you go on—you're doing a great job these days managing the ranch. I'm not working like I used to, and I'm glad I have you around." Dad smiled and reached to pat him on the back.

Austin's heart swelled, threatening to burst inside his chest. He glanced at his plate and then up to Dad again. "Thank you. Coming from you, well, that means a lot."

"Hey, you're my only son who knows how to fly a helicopter. Every time I ride out to the north pasture and see that machine sitting on the helipad, I get a little prouder."

"I'll probably get out to do a bit of night flying soon. I need to improve my license so I can carry passengers at night."

"You want to show off your skills to your siblings, do you?" He chuckled. "You know, I think we all miss them living at home. Peyton's doing a fine service for Oakville County these days, taking in homeless and needy boys from our area. I'm proud of him and Erica, too."

Mom smiled. "What did you want to discuss, son?"

Austin cleared his throat. "There're some problems in the north pasture. Mr. Whitlock pointed out that he'd seen lights in that direction. Also, someone or something is digging holes." Describing the situation in two sentences didn't seem to adequately explain the gravity of the issue.

Dad slowly turned his gaze to Mom and then frowned.

What was that look about? "Is there something I need to know, Dad?"

"No, son. Nothing definite. There have been rumors through the years … " He shook his head. "It's nothing."

"Rumors?" Austin tilted his head. "What kind of

rumors?"

Mom stood and gathered the plates from the table. "Let's talk about this another time, shall we? Your father is tired, and I know you are too, honey." She patted his hand.

Austin clenched his teeth. Dad was obviously thinking of something, some event that had happened years ago. "Another time, when? Is there something I need to know?"

Dad nodded his head. "Your mother is right. Another time."

Chapter Three

Tuesday morning, Willow settled into the driver's seat of her van. Since the results of Jack's nasal swab came in yesterday, she needed to treat the stallion as soon as possible.

She turned toward the county road leading to the Ford ranch. Memories of the first time she paid a call on Jack came rushing back.

Jack's owner had turned his gaze toward her, his green eyes with flakes of gold staring at her. Those same eyes she knew so well, eyes above a chiseled nose and perfectly shaped lips, transporting her back in time.

What had it been? A hallucination, or had she entered an alternate universe—far from the earth where she lived. No, it had all been too much. Seeing Jesse Lawson, whose funeral she had attended a year ago, standing in front of her that day had left her unconscious.

Willow drew in a deep breath. Things weren't

as they had appeared. Austin Ford and Jesse Lawson were two different men. And Jesse was dead.

The rolling hills and rocky layers of red clay and scrub bushes filled the terrain—so different from the green forests and coastal lands of California. But the hill country had its charms. She'd never regret moving to Oakville, Jesse's hometown as well as his mother's. Something Willow couldn't put off much longer—going to visit Emma Lawson.

Turning into the long drive onto the Ford Ranch, she spotted Austin approaching the horse barn. She pulled in front of the building and got out, ignoring the urge to hold her breath. No fainting this time.

She stiffened her shoulders, and her heart beat faster as she fixed her gaze on the man standing in front of her. *He's not Jesse. He's not Jesse.* After one more emboldened breath, she shook his hand. "I have the results of Jack's test."

Austin gave her a casual smile.

Did he perceive her as anyone other than the local veterinarian? She doubted it.

"Jack's waiting in his stall."

She followed Austin, admiring his wide gait, exactly like the man she'd loved. Even the tone and pitch of his voice. She fought the impulse to race to her van and drive away. She could hardly bear to confront the past staring her in the face.

Inside the barn, Jack stood in his stall, no luster in his eyes and his coat dull. No way she could leave the poor animal without treatment. "Hey, Jack. I've got some good medicine for you. You'll feel like your old self very soon." She wiped away the mucus in his nostrils and slipped the thermometer in his rectum. "I can tell without looking that Jack has a fever." After sixty seconds, she frowned. "His temperature is one hundred and two."

Austin petted Jack's neck. "I'm sorry, buddy, but you'll be fine soon. Now that the pretty doctor is here." He cleared his throat. "I mean the efficient veterinarian."

Austin's presence behind her sent chills up her spine. She grabbed one of the bars on Jack's stall to steady herself after the dizzy wave engulfed her. "If you'll hold his bridle, I'll give him his antibiotic."

While Austin held Jack's head steady, she slid the syringe up the side of the horse's mouth and dispensed the mixture into his cheek. She lifted up his head until he swallowed. "Good boy, Jack. A few more of these injections, and you'll be back to normal."

She glanced at Austin. "Jack will need to take these antibiotics two times a day for five days. I'm leaving you enough for the rest of the week. It might be convenient if you get one of the ranch hands to help you."

Austin focused on her with a look of quiet interest. Was he wondering if she was in her right mind after her bizarre behavior when she first visited the ranch? "I think I can handle that."

"Make sure you keep this area well-ventilated and his stall clean." She placed her stethoscope on Jack's left side against his rib cage to listen to his heartbeat. "His water and food should be changed twice a day."

Austin laughed and patted Jack's head. "You got it better than I do—all this attention."

Standing face to face with Austin, Willow allowed her curiosity to get the best of her once more. She set her gaze on the small mole near his left ear. Her mouth grew dry.

Austin opened his eyes wide. "Is there something wrong with me?" He touched his neck.

Willow wrapped her arms around her waist and shook her head. "No, I—may I ask, have you always had that place on your neck?"

Austin lifted his brow and stared at her. "As far as I know. Look, Dr. Lawson, is there something you need to tell me?"

She moved toward the door of the horse barn. "No, I'm sorry. There's nothing wrong with you. I'm sure you're a very nice person. I'm just not myself right now."

"Okay." He drew out the syllables and gave her another incredulous look, his eyes wide.

How much did she really want to tell him? He could lose respect for her or even dismiss her as his horse's vet. "I'll be back to check on Jack to see how he's doing in a week or so."

Willow waved goodbye and got in her van. She took off down the road and turned toward town, gripping the steering wheel. But when she returned to the Ford ranch, would she be free of the disturbing dreams that had bothered her for the last week? Dreams into which Austin Ford abruptly entered?

~

Austin lowered his napkin and rose from the supper table. "Hey, Dad. I'm doing some night flying, tonight. I need a couple more hours to finish my pilot's license."

"Great idea. My *Sheep Ranching Today* magazine speaks about the use of copters in herding animals and rescuing stranded sheep."

Seeing Dad accept some of the more up-to-date ranching practices pleased Austin. "I want to poke around over the north pasture—see if there's anything to what Mr. Whitlock said about seeing lights—that is if the so-called culprits are out now."

Dad sipped a cup of herbal tea. "Son, you know old Mr. Whitlock can be a trouble maker at times. If I were you, I'd ignore the man. Who would dig at night time out on the pasture? Sounds farfetched, don't ya think?"

Austin ran a quick hand through his hair. His father didn't put much stock in what the rancher said, but it didn't hurt to take a look. "You're probably right, but so I can have peace of mind tonight, I think I'll check it out."

Dad waved him off. "Do what you want."

Austin bit his lip. The other day Dad was all in favor of him flying. But now... Austin made his way to his helicopter resting on the helipad at the front edge of the north pasture. He did a quick preflight inspection, checking the rotor system, landing gear, and engine instruments. With a flick of the switches, the engine roared to life, and the rotors began to spin. He lifted the helicopter into the night sky.

For fifteen minutes, Austin flew the copter over the house and then the horse and sheep barns, and back to the west pasture. He turned in the other direction toward the north pasture.

Above the earth, the serene beauty of the nighttime landscape always made him feel closer to God. Moonbeams glistened, bouncing off Coyote Creek. How could their peaceful ranch be plagued with intruders? From his vantage point, the possibility seemed slight. Maybe Dad was right.

After five minutes, he glanced down at the edge of the north pasture, well-lit by the bright moonlight. Wasn't this the approximate area where Mr. Whitlock said he'd seen someone or something digging holes in the ground?

Austin decreased the main rotor pitch to allow the helicopter to fly closer to the ground. A minute later, he caught his breath. Dark, irregular patches were visible in the moonlight against the lighter terrain. Long shadows accentuated the depth and edges of the holes making them look more pronounced and eerie.

Austin hovered the copter over the area. Whitlock wasn't too far off when he said he saw lights. Someone had to dig these holes, and they likely did it at night. No animal could've made these uniform indentations in the ground.

Austin pivoted the helicopter and flew back to the ranch. He set the machine on the helipad again, an icy tremor cooling his bones. Should he say anything to Dad about this? No, he'd wait until after he inspected the area for himself.

~

The man's harsh voice cut through the air with a sharp, raspy tone, even surprising himself. "Someone in that copter spotted us. I told you to turn off your light and run for cover."

"I did, you idiot."

Anger overcame the man, and he grabbed the other's shirt and then released his hold. "Aw, what good does it do for us to get into it? Let's come back later tonight when the rancher's asleep."

Chapter Four

Willow escorted the dog's owner to the front door of her clinic. His shoulders slumped, the weight of grief evident in the way he cradled the lifeless form. Yet, no burden felt heavier than the sorrow she carried for the man who had lost his beloved companion.

She turned back to the examination room. Why did her tears flow so readily today? She'd lost patients from old age in the past. Merely a fact of life. Today was no different. The little Cocker Spaniel had led a long and happy life.

She dabbed at the tears dotting her cheeks. Death was never easy to abide, even among pets and animals. But losing a human you loved—how much worse. The grief of losing Jesse to cancer a year ago still sent waves of stabbing pain to her heart.

The thought had lingered in the back of her mind for long enough. She needed to visit Jesse's mom. Willow glanced at her appointment book. No more patients scheduled until later this afternoon. She locked the clinic door, headed for her van parked to the side of the building, and made her way to the established neighborhood.

Why had she procrastinated visiting Emma for these several months? Willow's office sat only a mile or so from here. She supposed she'd put it off because seeing Jesse's mother would rekindle a flood of memories she wasn't prepared to face. Thoughts of losing her husband still overwhelmed her.

Willow pulled up in front of the modest home with the wooden frames painted white. Regret hung over her like a dark shadow.

Then she straightened her shoulders at the realization. By not visiting Emma, Willow had only thought of herself. Maybe Willow's mother-in-law needed her support, something she should've offered sooner.

Towering oak trees formed a canopy over the street in front of the house. Rose bushes filled the flower beds. A variety of weeds which likely choked out any other flowers invaded the garden. Did the inside of the house need the work the yard did?

Willow gripped her hands into a tight ball as she tried to calm the crazy beating of her heart. She exited the van onto the sidewalk and trekked to the small porch. Perhaps she should've warned Emma she was coming.

Willow held her breath and tapped at the door,

wondering what seeing Emma again after a year would be like.

A few moments later, Willow tapped again.

"I'll be there in a moment."

Willow's stomach tightened as she heard her mother-in-law's voice.

The door squeaked opened. Emma clung to a walker, her long gray hair as neat and lush as a young woman's, hung to her shoulders. "Yes?"

Willow swallowed hard. "Emma, it's me."

Emma frowned, and then her mouth fell open. "Willow? Is it really you?"

"Please forgive me. I should've come sooner."

"Where are my manners?" Emma took a few labored steps backwards, maneuvering the walker around. "Please come in."

Willow stepped into the modest living room. A layer of dust covered the coffee table, and the hardwood floors appeared dull and covered with debris and footprints. Emma had always kept her house tidy when she and Jesse visited her in California. No doubt she struggled with the everyday tasks as a result of her arthritis.

Emma gave Willow a welcoming smile and spread her arms wide, moving her walker to one side.

Willow basked in the warmth of her mother-in-law's embrace. "I've missed you."

"And I've missed you, too."

Recollections of a mother-in-law who'd always

been an encourager and comfort came rushing back. "You're using a walker now? I remember when you said you were dealing with the early stages of rheumatoid arthritis."

"Yes dear. The disease has slowly progressed over the last couple of years. I have trouble getting around." She motioned to the couch. "But please, come and sit down. Tell me about yourself." She took a seat in the chair across from the couch. "I'd heard that Oakville had a new veterinarian named Dr. Lawson. I figured you'd come see me when you were ready." She glanced down at her legs. "As you can see, it's difficult for me to go anywhere."

Willow's cheeks burned, and she focused on her lap. "I'm so sorry, Emma. I know I should've come sooner, but I've been dealing with some difficulties."

"I'm sorry to hear that. What's wrong?"

Pressing her lips together, the thought struck her. She couldn't tell Emma about a local rancher who looked exactly like her son. "Oh, you know. The usual. Getting the local ranchers to trust a new veterinarian in town, hiring a parttime tech assistant—things like that."

"I wish you well, dear girl. I'd like to help you in any way I can."

Willow's heart warmed with the woman's kind words. "Thank you, and honestly, I thought seeing you again would bring back unbearable memories of Jesse's death." She swallowed hard. "But being with you again is wonderful."

Emma slowly moved to sit beside Willow, cupping her hand over Willow's. "Of course." She glanced away, ran her finger under her eye, and then turned to face her again. "I can't tell you how hard it's been for me, too. I never thought I'd see the day I'd outlive my son."

Willow placed her other hand atop Emma's. "But why return to Oakville? I remember you said you'd grown up here but moved to California before Jesse was born."

Emma rested against the couch pillows and breathed deeply as if lost in a fog of memories. She stared straight ahead for so long until Willow assumed she didn't want to answer. Then she spoke with a muted tone as if the words were caught in her throat. "As you know, Oakville is where I was born and where my parents lived. They died in a car accident shortly after Jesse's death and left me this house." She glanced toward the ceiling.

"I'm so sorry, Emma. I didn't know."

"I know you didn't. You experienced your own grief. I planned on telling you about the loss of my parents, and then I found it best to move here to this house. I couldn't add to your grief, and I wasn't handling my own very well." She glanced toward the ceiling. "I'm so sorry, dear, for not contacting you."

Emma's gentle voice, offered a soothing balm to Willow's grief. "I could say the same. I love you, Emma."

"I love you too." She leaned toward Willow, giving her a hug. "Unfortunately, I've prematurely slipped into old age. This arthritis has limited my ability to get around, making it harder to maneuver daily chores."

Love for her mother-in-law surged through her, filling her with warmth. "I'd like to come over to help you. Would you allow me to clean your house on occasion?" Willow chuckled.

Emma squeezed her eyes shut and then opened them, moisture glistening on her cheek. "Thank you. I'd love the opportunity to catch up."

"I'd like that, too. I'm feeling stronger these days, strong enough to share memories of Jesse."

"I'm happy to talk about my son any time you want." Emma patted her hand again. "How is your practice going these days? I remember in California how you loved caring for household pets."

Willow gave a nervous laugh paired with a wide smile. "Lately I've had the opportunity to treat larger animals. The local ranchers are calling me to check on their horses and sheep. The owner of the Ford Ranch asked me to come out and examine his horse, Jack. The poor fellow suffered from equine influenza."

"The Fords?" Emma's eyes opened wide, and she wrung her hands together.

"Yes, are you acquainted with them?"

"Who around here isn't? They're a prominent family in our community. Uh, which Ford did you deal with when you went to the ranch?"

An odd question for Emma to ask. "Austin Ford. Have you met him?"

Emma shifted on the couch and then rose and grasped her walker. "I'm a terrible hostess. Would you like a cup of coffee?"

Willow rose and walked a few steps toward Emma. "What is it? If I didn't know better, I'd think I said something about Austin Ford that made you uncomfortable." Had she spoken too quickly? She didn't want to alienate Emma. Not after they'd only begun to get reacquainted.

Emma turned to Willow with an expression she couldn't interpret. "No, dear. I'm sorry. I'm being silly."

Emma lumbered into the tiny kitchen and headed toward the counter where the coffeepot sat at one end.

No doubt, from the tightened grip on her walker and the frown on her face, the name Austin Ford had sparked a source of concern for Emma. If not distress, what was her mother-in-law not telling her?

~

Austin dug into his plate, tearing off a piece of golden, fried chicken, and dipping it into the thick gravy pooled beside a mound of buttery mashed potatoes. He washed it down with a sip of sweet tea.

"Betsy certainly has outdone herself tonight."

"She has, indeed." Dad smiled from his seat at the head of the table.

"All of the ingredients in the salad come from our garden. The lettuce, tomatoes, cucumbers." Across the table, Mom stabbed a bite of the greens and chewed.

From the adjoining table where the hands generally sat, Mac waved his fork. "I'm waiting for the pecan pie." He rolled his eyes. "I'll have to admit, Betsy's cooking is a little better than mine."

Mom laughed. "I think you're a great cook, Mac. You've certainly stepped in and helped, especially when Charlotte and Jace moved to their new home."

Austin glanced at his mother. "Have you heard from Jace and Charlotte lately?" He dabbed his mouth with his napkin. "Haven't seen my brother much this last year."

"Charlotte rarely has any extra time since she's trying to keep up with her one-year-old, but I'm hoping they can come to the annual fund raiser for our local boys' home." Mom's eyes sparkled. "I can't wait to see my newest grandbaby. Erica and Peyton should bring their toddler for a visit soon, I would expect."

Austin wouldn't mind seeing his little niece and nephew. Except for Tim, his other siblings had married and started families. But what about him? Would the day ever come when he'd get married and have a family? He swallowed a gulp of tea. He didn't have time to think about that right now. To talk to Dad about what he saw last night in the north pasture was more important. He turned his focus toward his father. "I took the helicopter up yesterday evening."

"And?" Dad took a bite of his crunchy pecan pie.

"Something's going on out there."

Dad placed his fork on his plate, obviously interested.

"I spotted what appeared to be holes in the ground and dropped down closer."

"What?" Dad furrowed his brow.

Mom sat up taller in her chair.

"I suppose I should've told you earlier, but I was occupied most of the day with the fence repair in the west pasture. But back to last night, the moonlight allowed me to see a little better than usual." Austin rubbed the back of his neck.

Dad lifted his hand in a stop position. "I'd like to go out there and take a look."

"All right. First thing tomorrow?"

Dad gave mom a quick glance and turned to Austin with the same expression he'd seen only a few nights ago when his father had avoided his question.

Mom frowned and patted Dad's arm. "Perhaps Austin needs to hear about the legend. There might be a connection."

Dad shrugged. "I really don't know how."

Mac rose from the table, probably clued into the fact a serious conversation was about to ensue. "I'll say good night now."

"Night, Mac." Austin blew out a frustrated breath and looked back at his parents. "What are you both trying to tell me? What legend?"

Dad cleared his throat. "Your great grandfather, Jeremiah Ford, purchased this ranch in the 1920s."

Austin raised his voice. "Dad, I know that. He was the original owner of Ford ranch."

"Just listen, son. The Great Depression began only a few years later. Your great grandfather was quite an entrepreneur and had amassed gold pieces. He'd seen how his parents had struggled when he was a child and never wanted that to happen to him and his family. As a bit of a hoarder, he decided to hide the gold. He decided to bury the treasure on the property because he'd heard tales of gangs of outlaws out of Ft. Worth who followed in the steps of Butch Cassidy and the Sundance Kid."

Dad sounded as if he was describing the plot of an old western. Austin widened his eyes. "Is the gold still there? Is that what the intruders were looking for? If so, how did they find out about something that happened years ago?"

His mother sipped another drink of tea. "You see, Jeremiah's son, Martin, your grandfather, had always heard rumors of the gold though Jeremiah didn't talk to anyone about it, except possibly his wife. He probably wanted to avoid exactly what happened—robbers in search of riches. The tales were spread far and wide in those days. Everyone in these parts had heard the same stories. Martin searched for years for the treasure."

Dad shook his head. "I did the same and never found anything. Your mother and I have come to the conclusion that if Jeremiah did indeed bury treasure on this ranch, it has either been confiscated by someone or it's buried somewhere so obscure no one can ever find it. It's lost to perpetuity."

"But then, how do we explain holes in the ground?"

"Son, the stories still run wild. People still believe there are precious metals buried here on the Ford ranch. When you were still a small boy, we had intruders with metal detectors sneak onto our land a couple of times. Same thing. They were looking for the gold pieces."

"And Grandfather Martin agrees?"

"Yes. We've all concluded the same."

Austin scratched his head. "How did the thieves know where to dig?"

"They probably hoped they'd make a lucky guess."

Austin furrowed his brows. "Or they could have some kind of a map?"

"That's possible, although I can't imagine where they'd get one." Dad rose from the table. "But if they're just guessing, and we don't catch those guys pretty soon, we might see holes popping up in the west pasture." Dad rose from the table. "We'll take a look out there tomorrow, but I don't think there's any need to call the sheriff at this point."

Austin shrugged. "One last question. Why haven't you mentioned this before?"

Dad wagged his head back and forth. "Because there was no point in it. If your grandfather and your father never found the treasure after all these years, what good would it do?" Dad folded his arms over his chest.

Austin picked up a couple of plates on the table to help Betsy clean up. Perhaps he should go into town to question his grandfather, but then Grandpa Martin couldn't tell him anything more than Dad did, could he?

Chapter Five

In the barn, Austin reached toward the sick sheep and gently lifted its eyelid. "I need to ask Willow to take a look at this one. The dark red is a good indicator of parasites."

Mac glanced up. "Willow is Dr. Lawson, the vet, I assume."

"Yeah, that's her."

Mac led the ewe to the separate pen they'd set up this morning. "Three animals for the vet to take a look at. Not too bad for the entire herd."

"Yep. I found signs of skin irritation on the other two. The health check took most of the day, but this is going to make Willow's work a lot easier. I'll see when she can come out."

Mac lifted both thumbs up. "Sheep inspection is over for another eight weeks."

Austin shed his plastic gloves and scrubbed his hands in the barn's sink. He glanced out the window toward the north pasture and frowned. He supposed

Dad would want to head out there before dinner. The sooner they uncovered what was going on the better.

Mac slapped him on the back. "Something on your mind, buddy? You seem preoccupied lately. Everything going okay with the ranch?"

Austin faced Mac. "Yeah, but we're having some issues in the north pasture." Mac was always so perceptive. He knew the workings of the ranch forward and backward.

"What happened?" Mac removed his bandana from his pocket and wiped his brow.

"I took the copter out there two nights ago. The moon was shining, but I wasn't expecting to see a bunch of holes, as if someone had been digging in the ground."

"Okay, now that's weird."

"Oakville has been a quiet community for as long as I can remember. Dad said there used to be rumors of treasure hunters looking for gold, but he's debunked the notion now. Even so, the fact that we're having disturbances at the ranch bothers me."

"If you need any help, let me know."

"I'll remember that. Mr. Whitlock from the ranch east of us has also seen lights. I plan to chat with him." He clasped Mac's shoulder. "Let's get some lunch."

In the dining room, Betsy's chicken sandwiches tasted like cardboard today. The mystery of the holes in the back pasture weighed on Austin more than he'd realized. After lunch, he headed to the shed where they kept the vehicles. A quick swing out to the north pasture should provide more information.

Dad waved from the front porch. "Hey, wait for me." He hopped into the passenger seat of the ATV. The dirt road delivered dust and grit into Austin's nostrils as the vehicle bounced across the terrain. Coughing a few times, he continued on to the eastern perimeter of the ranch.

The weight of concern pressed on his shoulders, yet the day unfolded in perfect beauty. Coyote Creek appeared in the distance. The small stream meandered between two stretches of lush grass.

Above, puffy white clouds drifted across the expanse of azure sky. Texas ash lined the back edge of the ranch. Beyond, the Jade Mountains sat on the horizon, white clouds gently caressing the jagged peaks. God's beauty always left him breathless.

Austin stopped at the edge of the Ford property and glanced at Dad next to him. "I believe this is where I saw the holes."

"All right. Park over there." Dad pointed to a clump of trees.

Austin's father would probably treat him like a kid when Austin was fifty. He restrained the comment he wanted to make and pulled over, stopping under the trees.

They got out of the ATV and trudged along the

tree line for several minutes and then back in the other direction.

Dad hmphed. "Son, I don't see anything other than grassy green pasture land. Are you sure you saw holes?"

Austin blew out a quick breath. He knew for a fact he'd seen something down here. But where? "I thought I saw the holes there along the edge of the property." Was he becoming paranoid? "Look, let's talk to Mr. Whitlock."

"You really think that would do any good? I don't trust him any farther than I can throw him."

Austin chuckled under his breath at Dad's expression.

"Maybe old man Whitlock has heard the rumor about the treasure and is doing the digging."

Austin shook his head. "Dad, that's crazy. Why would he say he'd seen lights if he's doing the digging?"

Dad ran a hand through his hair. "Who knows what's on that old rascal's mind?"

Austin knew his father well. His dad was getting impatient and ready to return to the ranch.

"Okay, son. Let's make a quick visit to the Whitlock ranch. If nothing else turns up, I say we forget about it."

Austin supposed Dad was right about discontinuing the search if they found nothing else. He jumped in the ATV and headed east toward the

Whitlock Ranch.

Ten minutes later, when they reached the rancher's pasture, the gate stood ajar. Which meant one thing. Mr. Whitlock had likely come onto their property and forgot to close the gate again. Surely, Betsy's father wasn't digging as Dad had said.

Austin drove through the gate and continued toward the Whitlock home. A hundred yards away, he spotted Whitlock, the reins of his horse looped around a tree branch and the rancher working on the adjacent section of fence. "Hey, Mr. Whitlock. Got a second?"

Mr. Whitlock turned, wiped his forehead with his bandana, and waved. "Hello neighbors. Austin. Mr. Ford. Everything okay today?"

Dad got out of the ATV, his boots hitting the ground heavier than usual. "Got something we need to talk to you about. Just wondering if you had seen any more lights in our back pasture?"

"Not since the last time I talked to Austin, but I found my old dog Ranger at the fence line with a broken leg last Monday. I suspect he fell into some kind of a hole. I took him to the new vet in town, and she patched him up. You know, Doctor Lawson."

Austin swallowed hard. Yea, he knew her. She'd fainted the day they'd met. "I'm sorry to hear about Ranger. If you have a second, do you mind showing me where you saw the set of holes? Is it the same place as the first time we rode out there?"

Mr. Whitlock wiped his brow with the back of

his hand. "Sure thing. I'm finished with this fence repair so I can take you now."

Austin followed in the ATV as Mr. Whitlock rode his horse through the open back gate and onto the Ford property.

The rancher reined his animal to a stop at the area beyond where Austin and Dad had searched only an hour ago. Betsy's father tied his horse to a tree and then tramped into a group of ash trees, his boots crunching last year's fallen leaves.

Austin caught his breath. Underneath the shade of the trees, the rich, brown soil was displaced where uneven mounds of dirt rimmed the holes. Some two feet and others five or more feet deep. Some were freshly dug while others were filled with fallen sticks and limbs.

"This must be the spot I saw last night from the helicopter."

"Well, son. You're right about the holes. And I don't believe any animal has done this."

Sweat rolled down Austin's neck. "Do you feel like we need to get Sheriff Banks involved?"

Dad paced a few turns toward one of the openings in the ground and back. "At this point, I don't know how we can call the sheriff out here because we have holes in our pasture. Let's keep an eye on things." Dad gripped his fists into tight balls. "But this makes me so cotton picking mad. If this damage is the result of trespassers, we'll discover who it is, mark my words."

Austin liked Dad's positive attitude. "I pray you're right." At least now, Austin knew Dad had seen the damage for himself. He turned to Mr. Whitlock. "I'm sorry about Ranger breaking his leg. We'll get to the bottom of this, sir."

Mr. Whitlock scratched his head. "I suppose I better keep Ranger close to the ranch."

"Good idea." If these disturbances were made by intruders, were they looking for the legendary gold? One story he wouldn't share with the neighbor at this moment.

~

Willow parked her van in front of the horse barn and stepped out. She glanced around for any sign of Austin. No one seemed to be about so she opened the side door to the building where Jack recuperated. The aroma of fresh hay told her he was getting good care.

The horse lapped up water from the trough and then sneezed. His eyes dull, he switched his head from side to side as if trying to rid his nose of mucus.

"Hey Jack, how you feeling?" No doubt he needed another round of antibiotics though it would be best to check with Austin as to when he'd administered Jack's last dose.

The squeaking of the door alerted her that someone had arrived at the barn.

"Dr. Lawson." Jesse's soft, masculine voice

resounded in her ears. Chills raced down her back. No. Not Jesse. How could it be? She whirled around.

"I didn't know you were coming today." Austin towered over her like Jesse had. "But I'm glad you did. I need you to check on some sheep."

"Sorry, I didn't call ahead of time. I had another patient down the road and figured I'd stop in to see Jack on my way. I want to give him a stronger dose of antibiotics."

"I finished the last of Jack's medication you prescribed this morning."

"Good." She held out the container with his new, stronger antibiotics. "Here's his next round."

Willow wiped the horse's nose with an old rag sitting near the water trough. "Don't worry. You're going to be as good as new pretty soon." Did the animal understand her? Somehow, she believed he did.

She patted Austin's arm. "And you don't worry about Jack. I think we'll see complete improvement in a couple of weeks. You said you needed me to check on some sheep?" Again, Willow couldn't restrain the urge to stare at Austin. His lips, his hair, his eyes—as if Jesse had returned from the grave. The threatening dizzy waves rushed over her. She grasped the side of Jack's stall.

"Dr. Lawson, Willow." Austin reached to steady her. "Are you okay? I hope you're not going to faint again. Must be something about me that bothers you." He shrugged.

"No, I'm sorry. I, er …" She caught her breath as the notion popped into her mind. Maybe she could get to know Austin a little better to discover if he was anything like Jesse. His personality, his likes and dislikes. "Do you mind if we talk for a short while?"

"Sure. Do you want to go out back to the swing? Afterward, we can check on the sheep. I did a health check and have three in isolation. I suspect an eye infection on one of them."

"I'll be happy to." Though the handsome rancher might misunderstand her intentions, she had to know more about him. She had to discover why he was the exact image of Jesse—his build, the way he walked, his voice.

"The swing's out back behind the patio." He laughed. "My sister and one of our ranch hands, Peyton Langley, used to sit out there for hours before they got married. They had a lot to talk about, I guess."

More like they were falling in love out there on the swing. She grinned and followed Austin along the paved road around the front and side of the elegant ranch house. At the edge of the beautifully landscaped backyard, a wooden swing for two hung under an umbrella-shaped elm.

With an odd look on his face, perhaps because he couldn't imagine what she wanted to talk about, he pointed to the seat. "Is this okay?"

Willows heart pounded harder as the rancher edged down by her side, brushing her arm with his warm one. She fought against the bizarre notion. Jesse who'd passed away months ago, took a seat beside her. Austin even had his same scent. She had to get to the bottom of this. For her own sanity.

"Did you want to talk about Jack? Or the sheep?"

Willow couldn't help but giggle under her breath. "Not about the animals this time."

Austin peered at her. "Honestly, sometimes women baffle me. You included."

The cool breeze blowing under the elm cooled Willow's face. "I feel the same about men most of the time. But let me try and explain."

"Yes, that might help." Austin's smile drew her in, as if he had secrets of his own to share.

Willow's cheeks warmed. She hoped the good-looking guy wouldn't think she was a flirt. She took a breath and forced her lips to form the words. "You remind me of someone I knew. You may think this an odd question, but what kind of books did you read when you were a kid?"

Austin's eyes narrowed as if he tried to make sense of her question. "Let's see, I used to read the Hardy Boys."

Willow caught her breath and stared at him. *Same as Jesse.* "What was your favorite vegetable?"

Austin shook his head and laughed. "I suppose I used to love the way my mom prepared asparagus."

Hmm. Jesse always wanted her to fix Brussel

sprouts. Nevertheless, he also liked vegetables. "And your favorite color?"

"That's easy. Green like the pasture in summer."

Willow furrowed her brow. *Jesse loved blue.* Their likes and dislikes didn't completely match up, but no two individuals would be exactly alike. Jesse and Austin were two people who just happened to look a lot alike—no big deal.

~

Austin took Willow's hand in a firm grip as she maintained constant eye contact. If he were to guess, she struggled to process what he'd said. "Are you okay?" He'd never seen anyone react quite like her when he told them he'd read the Hardy Boys and liked asparagus. So many things about Willow he didn't understand.

"You'll have to forgive me. My life hasn't been the same lately." She twisted her hands into knots.

Austin peered at the young woman—her creamy tanned skin, full lips, and slightly slanted brown eyes. "Now it's your turn. Tell me something about yourself."

"I, I ..."

Willow's stammering reply clued him into the fact she wasn't comfortable talking about herself. "I grew up in California. My mother was Polynesian, and my father was from Michigan."

"Was?"

"Yes." She stared toward the mountains in the distance. "After I graduated from vet school, they died in an earthquake."

Austin restrained the urge to brush a long strand of her hair from her face and hold her hand again. "I'm so sorry."

Her posture softened, and a quiet calm seemed to settle over her. "I've suffered more loss than I want to think about. But the Lord has been gracious in giving me peace."

He needed to divert the conversation from the loss of loved ones. "Since you chose to become a veterinarian, you must have always had a love for animals."

"Yes. I remember when I was eight, I tried to nurse a baby bird back to health when it fell out of a nest. The bird survived, and one day, I had the privilege of seeing it fly away. After school, I worked as an associate vet in California until I came here to set up my own practice." She dropped her gaze to her lap.

Austin didn't need to ask any more questions. Though he figured she was used to being around him by now, he didn't want to take the chance of her passing out again. He took a breath and gazed toward the east pasture.

Behind him in the direction of the helicopter pad, the sound of a tree limb breaking and a rustling of leaves caught his attention. Likely, a deer rummaging for food. He turned to the woman beside him who only moments ago seemed to wrestle with something that triggered a strong emotion in her.

Her hands shook. "I have a few more questions. I know you probably grew up on this ranch, but what did you enjoy doing in your spare time?"

Willow was obviously going somewhere with all of this. But where? He scratched the back of his neck. "Let's see. I used to love photography. I had a Cannon Powershot, a digital point-and-shoot pocket camera. I was always on the lookout for a location that would make a good picture."

Willow searched his face, and then furrowed her brows.

"Look, Willow. There's a point to all these questions? I'd like to know."

Willow ran her hands through her long, dark hair and rose from the swinging chair. "I can't. At least not now. Please try to understand."

Austin eased himself up from the swing, taking a few tentative steps toward the sheep barn. There was no point in pushing her for more than she was willing to share—it might send her spiraling again. "All right. Fair enough. I'm here if you want to discuss the issue."

"Thanks for understanding. Shall we check on those sheep now?"

Would he ever discover what was going on with the new veterinarian?

Chapter Six

Willow stepped out of her apartment building into the warmth of the summer morning. She breathed in the scent of zinnias and fresh-cut grass and paused a moment, feeling the sunshine on her skin. Why not relish the out-of-doors a little longer and walk to the clinic today?

Memories flooded her mind with the many warm summer evenings in California, when she and Jessie had strolled hand in hand after supper. They'd talked about their hopes and dreams for the future—a home with a swimming pool, a golden doodle someday, and maybe a child in a few years.

Willow let out a soft sigh. He never had the chance to see those dreams come true. The Lord had taken him while he was still so young. Though she sometimes questioned God's plan, she always reminded herself that He never made a mistake.

Mistakes. She prayed she hadn't made a mistake

by asking Austin so many questions, but she had to know how similar or dissimilar he was from Jesse. She needed more clues about why Austin looked so much like her late husband. Was it a coincidence? A fluke as she'd concluded the other night? Or on second thought—had they been related?

Ambling down the five-blocks to her vet's office, she enjoyed the unhurried pace. At the front entrance to the clinic, she pulled out her key and unlocked the door.

Inside, she glanced around and then blinked, as if that could change the scene before her. She froze, her mind racing to make sense of what she saw. She closed her eyes and opened them again, but the devastation remained.

In the front office, chairs sat on their sides. Her diploma, glass shattered and frame smashed, lay on the floor.

She caught her breath, again trying to understand what had happened. She took two cautious steps into the lab, her pulse quickening with every movement. The fluorescent lights flickered above, casting long, uneasy shadows across the room. Willow's stomach twisted in knots, dread rising like a wave about to crash over her.

Bottles that once contained medications for her patients lay upside down on the floor in broken pieces. Resting sideways on the table, her microscope was cracked. The X-ray machine was detached from the ceiling brace and cast to one side on the floor.

With both hands, she clasped her cheeks as a lump formed in her throat. Her laptop lay on the floor beneath her desk, the computer's screen smashed and data likely lost.

She stared at the desk's surface. Something else was missing. She closed her eyes to remember.

The framed picture of Jesse. The frame lay smashed on the floor but no photo in sight.

Willow took a breath, one that sounded more like a sob, as she recalled the image she had of Jesse from a few months before he passed. This wasn't merely a break-in—it was sabotage. Tears rolled down her face, her eyes burning. She moaned, "Dear Lord, what has happened?"

Struggling to breathe, she glanced up at the back wall. Words written with red spray paint sent an icy chill down her back.

Go back home. You're not wanted here.

Her hand shaking, she pulled out her cell phone and dialed 9-1-1. "Please send Sheriff Banks to Dr. Lawson's office. There's been a break in."

In only moments, the sound of sirens announced the arrival of the officials. She jerked her head toward the office window and looked out.

The sheriff's car slid to a stop and two officers raced toward the front door. "Are you all right, ma'am?"

Forcing back the tears, Willow directed the

police officer and his deputy to her lab. "I'm okay, but my clinic is not. My equipment is destroyed." Now was not the time to get hysterical. She gulped a deep breath and pointed at the wall. "I don't understand the meaning of those words. Vandals have wrecked my property."

Sheriff Banks studied the wall a moment and scratched his head. "Do you have any idea why someone would want you to leave?"

Willow shook her head. "No, I can't imagine. I haven't made any enemies here. I've only treated the town's animals to the best of my ability." She exhaled, hoping to rid herself of the growing frustration.

"Don't worry, ma'am." The sheriff pulled out a notepad and a pen. "Oakville is a small town. We'll get to the bottom of this. I assume you don't have an alarm system."

An involuntary gulp caught in her throat. "No, I don't. I see now that was a mistake."

The sheriff glanced at the other officer. "See if you can lift fingerprints while I talk to Dr. Lawson."

For the next half hour, Willow racked her brain trying to figure out who could have done such a thing. "I can't understand what's going on." She inspected the spray-painted words on the back wall again. "Why would someone want me to leave Oakville?"

The official jotted something on his notebook. "I can't understand why anyone would want a competent veterinarian to leave our area. We need your services."

Austin. He'd lived here all his life. Maybe he'd have some ideas. Besides, she needed his support right now. Willow searched her back pocket for her cell phone. "If you don't mind, I'm going to call a friend."

Her voice squeaked when Austin said hello. "I need you to come to the clinic as soon as possible. Something terrible has happened."

~

Austin's heart hit his stomach like a heavy stone when he glanced around Willow's office. The unthinkable had happened, Willow's brand-new clinic destroyed, but why? What mystified him even more were the strange red words. What did the culprit mean that Willow should leave Oakville?

"We'll be in touch, Dr. Lawson." The sheriff took a few notes and then paused on his way out the door with the deputy. "Oakville is considered to be one of the safest towns in Texas. I never thought I'd hear myself saying this, but keep your doors locked and don't hesitate to call if you believe you might be in danger. We'll patrol your house twenty-four seven."

Willow shook her head. "Thank you, Sheriff." She batted at a tear on her cheek.

She looked so small and distraught. Her veterinarian practice likely put on hold until she could replace her equipment. What would she do to support herself? How could he help her?

Austin ground his teeth hard. The more he thought about someone who would threaten her, the more he wanted to see the intruders into her office brought to justice. "I'm so sorry about this. Look, I can round up some folks on Saturday to at least help you get this place cleaned up. I'm pretty sure my sister, Erica, and her husband, Peyton, can come over. Mac, our ranch hand, could probably help, too."

Willow sniffed and then her shoulders shook as if the grief had overcome her.

Austin gave into what he'd vowed he wouldn't and slowly slid his arms around her. "Shh, Willow. I'm here for you."

She pulled back, her face stained with tears and whispered. "I need your strength—and God's right now. I'm not sure where my future is taking me."

"Speaking of the Lord, would you like to come to church with me and my family on Sunday? I realize things are pretty tough right now, but there's nothing God can't handle."

Willow nodded. "Thank you. I'd like that."

Austin slid one arm over Willow's shoulders. "At least let me take you to breakfast. We can talk about what's happened and any decisions you need to make. Maybe we can hash over some possibilities and get an idea of what's going on. And who made that threat."

"In the last hour, I've asked myself that question

a hundred times."

He stopped and gripped her hand. "There's something I haven't told you."

Her gaze lifted to his, uncertainty flickering in her eyes.

"We've had some disturbances in the north pasture lately. Someone has intruded on our property and begun digging holes.

Willow leaned against the only item in the room which seemed to have escaped the culprit's hands, the lab table. "Yes, I heard about the mysterious holes. A few weeks ago, your neighbor, Mr. Whitlock, brought his dog, Ranger, to the clinic to take care of his broken leg. He said Ranger had escaped through the fence and fallen into some holes in your back pasture."

"Word gets around fast in a small community." Austin stared at the ugly red words again.

Willow's slender shoulders slumped. "There's one thing I know for sure. Replacing all of the equipment will take thousands of dollars, and dealing with my insurance company will take time. For now, I have to find another source of income. But what kind of job could I get?"

Chapter Seven

After attending church, Willow followed Austin to the backyard behind the ranch house. His gait, his frame, so like Jesse's. She'd asked the question a million times. Would she ever understand how two men could look so much alike? Different last names, different mothers, different fathers. There's no way Austin could be related to Jesse. And yet—Austin was the exact copy of her late husband.

Austin paused and grasped her hand. "I hope you liked the service today. I've attended this church since I was a kid. I suppose if you haven't gone to a cowboy church before, you might feel out of place. Most of the congregation shows up in Western wear." He snickered.

"I felt at home, but you're right. I've never seen a pastor wear a cowboy hat and boots. The scripture he read was meant for me. 'God is our refuge and strength, a very present help in trouble.'"

Austin's eyes softened, glistening with what she could only describe as compassion. "You're going to get through this, Willow. My family is here to help wherever we can."

"Thank you." Willow cleared the frustration from her throat. "Not all families take the time to bless newcomers. And thank you for all the help yesterday getting the clinic cleaned up. I enjoyed meeting Erica, Peyton, and Mac."

Austin smiled. "When you come to know the Ford family better, you'll discover my parents and siblings care about others, especially those in need. I suppose it has something to do with our faith." Love radiated from Austin's smiling face. "You know, my parents throw a huge barbecue fundraiser for the local boys' home in Oakville every year."

She gave Austin a wide smile. "You're blessed to have a family like them."

The aroma of grilled hamburger meat pulled her away for a moment. Her stomach growled.

A long rectangular table sat on the deck facing the well-kept, lush lawn shaded by oak and maples. The table was laden with grilled hamburgers, condiments, hot dogs, bowls of potato and pasta salad, a huge fruit bowl, and pitchers of lemonade.

Austin guided her closer, his hand on her back.

She remembered. Jesse possessed that same faith in God, for which Willow couldn't be more grateful. The best part—she knew where he was today.

The family had begun to gather near the table, along with Chet and Pete.

Austin removed his Stetson, wiped his brow, and dropped his hat down again on his head. "Your assistant, Chet, showed up here when he was seventeen. Dad hired him as a ranch hand. Though we had some problems at first, Dad gave him a chance."

The good news lifted her heart. Others had recognized Chet for the dependable young man he was. "Your family has been a good influence on him. As you know, he's working toward a degree as a veterinarian tech and someday as a full-fledged vet."

Then she realized the truth. Willow gripped Austin's arm. "Because I won't be in business for a while, Chet will be out of a job. But God willing, I'll be back to work before too long." Who was she kidding? It would take months to get her practice up and running.

"Chet will find another job to see him through. I have no doubt. Or he can work on the ranch again with his brother Pete."

Mrs. Ford emerged from the kitchen backdoor with a large basket of buns. "Okay, everyone. Come to the table. We're ready to eat." She glanced at Willow. "I'm so glad you could make it today."

Austin poked her side and grinned. "See, I told you. The Fords care about you." He removed his hat and bowed his head.

After Mr. Ford asked God's blessing on the food, Austin held a chair for her and sat in the next one.

Mrs. Ford at the other end smiled. "All right, folks. I believe you all know this young lady, Dr. Willow Lawson—all except for Mr. Langley and Pete. Willow, this is Peyton's father who helps run Horse Haven Boys' Ranch, and Pete is Chet's brother."

Mr. Langley smiled. "We were blessed to have a free day as the boys' went for visits in the various homes of church members."

Willow smiled. "Nice to meet you both." As the bowls were passed around, she served herself a juicy hamburger patty, pasta salad, and a portion of the fruit concoction.

Fifteen minutes later, the conversation died down. Mr. Ford glanced around the table. "Can I count on your help this year with the fundraiser barbecue?"

Chet grinned through a bite of potato salad. "Are you kidding, Mr. Ford? I might never have met up with my brother Pete if you hadn't held the event. Count me in."

Austin lowered his voice and leaned toward Willow. "That's quite an interesting story."

Willow nodded and then sampled the food on her plate. Near the table, the colorful flower beds burst with color, lifting her spirit and her heart. Warmth spread through her chest. Despite her feeling of loneliness when she first arrived, here at the ranch she enjoyed the protection and peace the Fords offered.

Mr. Ford clinked his water glass with his fork. "We've made a change this year." Austin's father grinned at Willow and then winked. "My wife and I had a talk last night, and we'd like to give you thirty percent of the proceeds toward opening up a new office. Through the years, we've donated the funds to a worthy cause—the boy's home. The break-in was unfortunate event and of no fault of your own. We consider your practice a great benefit to our community and want to help you."

Once again, tears welled in Willow's eyes. She took a deep breath, trying to mask the emotions stirred by her gratitude for this caring family.

Erica bounced her baby on her lap. "I love that idea. I'll be here for this year's fundraiser, as well."

Mrs. Ford grinned. "Willow, in the time being, I hope you'll still make ranch calls. Our Jack and the sheep need you."

Willow smiled. She'd thought about that. Just because her lab equipment was gone didn't mean she couldn't use the remaining items she'd stored in her van. She could drive to the ranches and perform routine procedures. "I'll definitely make house calls for any local rancher who needs me. In the meantime, I heard that there's an opening at the Oakville Pet and Animal Feed Store. I plan to apply tomorrow. I could live on my savings and the money I get on ranch and house calls, but I don't want to deplete my bank account."

Austin chuckled. "You're likely overqualified for that job."

Her cheeks heated. "I'll be grateful for any

position I can get right now to see me through for a while."

Though this family welcomed Willow, why did she have the feeling that there was much more to discover concerning these generous people?

~

Austin untied his apron and helped Willow out of hers and then hung them on the hook by the stove. "Betsy appreciated our help since she usually doesn't work on Sundays."

"Your mom deserves a break as well. I was glad to wash a few dishes, especially since Erica and Peyton had to take their fussy baby home." She laughed. "That little one probably got tired after all the attention."

Austin grinned at Willow, trying to disguise his pounding pulse. Why she made him feel this way, he didn't know. "Since I've never had a kid, I have no idea what to do for them. Peyton's getting the hang of fatherhood, I'm pretty sure. When I first met him, he was as clueless about babies as a cowboy at a ladies' tea party. Erica—I think it came naturally for her."

Willow covered her mouth and giggled. "You haven't been a father yet, but you're a horse owner. The animal can't tell you what's wrong, just like a baby, but you know him so well, you can figure it out. It's no different with a small child."

"If you say so." Austin chuckled. "Hey, would

you want to go out to the north pasture? I'd like your opinion on the holes and disturbances out there. For one thing, you can see the spot where Ranger broke his leg."

She nodded. "Sure. Let's go."

Austin pulled the ATV around to the back of the house, and Willow climbed in next to him. The May sun warmed his skin as the vehicle bumped and jostled them. He wiped his brow with his checkered bandana. In a couple of months, they'd feel the full force of the Texas heat.

Austin circled the section of the pasture at the perimeter of the ranch where he first thought he'd seen the lights. "As you can see, nothing seems to be disturbed here. But I'll show you where we found the holes. Did I tell you I fly a small helicopter?"

"No." She widened her eyes, perhaps impressed with his intentional bragging. "I'd like to take a ride one of these days."

"You've got it. But the night I flew over this area, I saw nothing as you can tell here." He turned the ATV toward the east and the Whitlock ranch. Within moments, he drove up to the piece of land loaded with holes, some deep, others shallow. "Here's where Ranger broke his leg."

Nestled within a small grove of oak trees, the area extended almost to Mr. Whitlock's fence.

Mr. Whitlock. Austin had just about dismissed the notion that his neighbor had been responsible for the holes.

Willow bent down to examine one of the unusual places in the earth. "Do you or your father have any idea about who was out here?"

"No, not really." Should he share the family rumor? He explicitly trusted her. "Look, Willow. We don't talk much about it, but there's a rumor passed down since my great grandfather's day about hidden treasure. That's the only possible conclusion we can come to." Austin described the old tale about his great grandfather Jeremiah.

"So, it's possible someone is looking for gold."

Austin nodded. "It appears that way."

Willow took a few steps, nosing around each hole. "Whoever made these indentions in the earth certainly didn't care about being consistent. Nor did he or she dig down very deep in some of them. I wonder what the objective was. And why now after all these years?"

"I suppose if I knew the answers to those questions, I'd be a lot closer to identifying the culprit or perhaps culprits." Austin breathed deeply to catch a breath, the windless day offering little relief.

"I wish I could be of more help. But I have a feeling, you'll discover who they are. Did you notify the sheriff?"

"No. Dad wants to wait until we have a bit more evidence."

As if the wind had begun to blow again, rustling

reverberated in the bushes behind the trees.

Willow gripped his arm. "Austin." Her voice held a note of fear. "There's no breeze today. What made the noise over there in the bushes? Could it be a coyote?"

He turned toward the area. "Maybe, but I doubt it. Stay here for a minute." He patted his revolver tucked into the holster at his waist and passed through the trees, pushed his way into the bushes, and came out on the other side.

A couple of more rustling sounds and then everything was quiet. Nothing.

Was it their imaginations or had both he and Willow heard the sound of someone out there. He dashed back the way he'd come. Stupid move, leaving Willow there alone. Through the bushes and then the trees, he shouted. "Willow, are you okay?"

Silence. Austin's heart pounded harder. Had someone attacked Willow? Now running hard, he arrived at the spot where he'd left her. "Willow, where are you?"

Moments later, Willow wound her way through the trees on the west side of the area. "Austin, I heard you shouting. I hope everything's okay."

He rushed to her, pulling her into his arms. "You're okay. That's all that matters." His neck warmed, and he took a few steps back. "I'm sorry, er, I was worried about you."

Her sweet smile filled her face. "Did you see

anything?"

"Nothing back that way."

She ran her hand over his, looking into his eyes as if she'd known him all her life and cared deeply for him. "I can't wait any longer. There's something I need to tell you."

~

Willow couldn't hide the truth from Austin another moment. Nor could she hide the truth from herself. She never thought it would happen, but it had. Austin's touch made her heart pound. Was it because she imagined Jesse's arms were around her?

His eyes searched hers, no doubt wondering what she had to say. "Sure. Do you want to sit in the ATV?"

"Yes." Willow slid into the passenger seat next to Austin, fiddling with a thread on her jeans.

"That frown on your face tells me it must be serious." Once again, Austin held her hand, and her pulse took off.

"I didn't want to tell you for a while, but I think it's time." Willow's mouth went dry.

"All right." His eyes locked on hers. "But why now?"

"Because, er, I suppose I'm finding I have …." Why was this so hard? How could she tell him she'd begun to see him as more than a patient's owner. She swallowed hard. "I was married before, and my husband passed away a little over a year ago from cancer."

Austin froze as if trying to process what she'd said. "I'm so sorry, Willow. That must've been difficult—having lost your parents and your husband."

"It was, but with God's strength, I began to heal."

He smoothed his hand over hers. "Why were you reluctant to tell me? It's no shame when someone loses a spouse."

"Yes, thanks for understanding." She brushed a strand of her hair from her cheek, giving herself time to form the words. "But I haven't told you all of the story."

He tilted his head to the side. "Go ahead."

She swallowed hard. "You are an identical copy of Jesse."

Austin smiled. "Willow, everyone has someone that looks like them."

She placed two fingers on his lips. "No, you don't understand. I mean you look exactly like him, down to that mole you have on your neck—on the opposite side from his. Tell me something. What hand do you write with?"

"My right."

"He was left-handed." She took a deep breath. "Your boyhood interests were the same as his. Your tone of voice and the way you walk. It's uncanny."

Austin stared at her as if she'd arrived from another planet. "You said his name is Jesse...Jesse Lawson. Tell me more about him."

"I met him in California after I graduated from vet school. His father had passed away, but I got to know his mother, Emma. She was a sweet woman."

"What was his profession?"

"He was an accountant."

Austin stared straight ahead, lowering his voice. "I always wanted to be an accountant but decided not to work outside the family business. These days, I can use my ability with numbers and finances here at the ranch."

Willow's skin tingled. Telling Austin now made it all the more real. She stared at his face, and a chill rushed her spine. She pinched her arm. *This man isn't Jesse, this man isn't Jesse. Lord, help me. I think I'm losing my mind.*

A warm hand covered hers. "Willow, are you okay?"

She opened her mouth, but no words emerged. She sighed. Austin was so like her husband. Temptation began to press on her—to believe that Jesse had returned from the dead to be a part of her life again. But no. People didn't ordinarily rise from the dead—except, of course, Jesus Christ, God's Son. "I'm sure this is hard to hear. At first, I didn't want to tell you, but now I can't keep it a secret any longer." She gripped both hands in her lap.

Austin studied her face, her brows, her lips, her chin. "What are you trying to tell me?"

Willow took the risk. In moments, he'd know what her heart had said for days now. "I am beginning to find feelings for Austin Ford who is an exact copy of my husband, Jesse, and I'm so confused."

Chapter Eight

The man stuffed the wad of tobacco between his cheek and lower gum to draw out the minty flavor. The sticky substance dried out his mouth, but the buzz of nicotine was worth it.

The other man scowled. "Your breath stinks and that stuff is turning your teeth brown."

The man slapped at the air in the direction of the other. "Aw, shut up. You better be glad I've got brains. We're going to get rich someday."

"I suppose. That last move over at the clinic was risky, though."

"Listen, it's like I told you. We had to warn the vet that she'll never find that gold before us. She needs to know we're trailing her. She needs to know we mean business, and she'll never win. Even if she is in good with that Austin Ford."

"One thing is weird, though."

"What?"

"That Ford creep looks just like Jesse."

"Hey, get quiet. I think I hear something."

The second man whispered. "We better get out of here. They may see us."

~

Austin's head spun. She had feelings for him? His heart raced, and he used every ounce of restraint he had not to pull her close and place his lips on hers. He was falling for her, too, and he never dreamed she'd care about him. What's more, there'd been another on this earth who was his exact duplicate. He clenched his jaw. Did she have feelings for him because he reminded her of her deceased husband—someone to replace Jesse?

In the north pasture, a lark's melodious call from a tree above soothed his tense nerves—and his doubts. He reached for her chin and turned her lips toward him and whispered what his heart spoke, not his head. "I don't want to rush anything, but this guy has feelings for you, too."

She turned in her seat and clung to him. "Oh, Austin, I don't know what to say. I'm not sure where this is going."

"Me, either. Let's take it slow. The Lord will show us." Austin drew her to him and wrapped his arms around her. Too soon for a kiss. Hadn't he said they'd take it slow? He repeated the warning to himself, hoping that the part of him who didn't want to take it slow would listen.

With a deep breath, Austin soaked up the quiet and the presence of the exquisite, gentle woman beside him. He listened to her smooth breathing and then heard another sound.

Whispers and the sound of broken branches disturbed him. A coyote or a couple of deer? No, those animals didn't whisper. He sat up and started the engine. "Let's get back to the house." An unsettling feeling gnawed at him, as if the trees themselves concealed hidden threats within their shadows.

Chapter Nine

The next evening, Austin finished the piece of cherry pie, dabbed his mouth with his napkin, and pushed back from the dinner table. "Mom, Dad, can you meet me out on the back deck. I have something to discuss with you." Still processing the news about Willow's husband, he couldn't deny the urge to confide in his parents.

Mom tilted her head to one side as if weighing the possibilities of what he'd say. "Of course, honey. Your father and I will be right out."

Willow's news about her deceased husband had stayed with him all Sunday, and now the need to get it out almost overcame him.

Austin sank into the couch opposite the easy chair on the deck. Talking to his parents about relationships with women wasn't something he usually did, but now he needed their perspective. Perhaps they could offer clarity about what had transpired. And he needed their reassurance. Maybe they'd have a clue as to why someone would look exactly like him.

Austin rested his head on the couch pillow and took a deep breath of the earthy scent of fresh hay mingled with the warm smell of the horses. To the west, the sun slipped under the horizon, gracing the evening sky with hues of gold and silver. Despite the peace engulfing him, would this conversation shed light on his questions?

Mom relaxed on the couch next to Austin. "From the look on your face, I'd say something pretty big is bothering you."

"But there's nothing that the Fords and the Lord can't handle together." Dad patted Austin's back and sank in the chair across from them.

"Thanks for the reminder." Dad seemed to have changed after Erica got married, possibly acknowledging that his youngest son could handle more responsibility. Maybe semi-retirement had helped to prompt that attitude.

Mom, in her jeans skirt and white blouse, crossed one leg over the other. "Austin, before we get started, I'd like to tell you I'm so grateful you're taking more responsibility for running the ranch." She snickered. "You never know when Dad and I might retire."

"Yes son. I echo your mother's words, and if this is about what's been going on in the back pasture, we'll get to the bottom of it, I promise."

"I have no doubt, but that's not why I asked to talk with you both."

"You know you can discuss anything you want with us." Mom giggled. "Is it something about the new vet that's treating Jack?"

Austin couldn't restrain his chuckle. Leave it to a mother's intuition. "What makes you say that?"

A soft pink glow filled Mom's cheeks. "I see the way that you look at her—with more than casual interest. To tell you the truth, she looks at you in the same way."

Dad grumbled. "What are you two talking about? I didn't notice them giving each other crazy looks."

Mom threw her head back and laughed.

"Yeah, Mom." Austin laughed again. "With more than casual interest? What does that even mean, anyway?"

Mom clasped two hands on her hips. "You men are all clueless. Don't you know when two people are in love?"

Dad eyed Austin. "I think your mom is teasing us now."

Heat filled Austin's neck. Were his feelings about Willow noticeable? Was he actually in love? "Yeah mom, what gives?"

Mom patted his hand. "I was having a little fun with you. Go ahead with what you wanted to say."

Mom had likely come closer to the truth than

she knew. Which made the situation with Willow and her deceased husband even more complicated. He ran his hand through his hair. "Okay, I admit I do have feelings for the new vet, and I'm pretty sure she feels the same about me."

"So, what's the problem?" Dad stared him down.

Austin shifted in his seat. There was no comfortable answer right now. He had to get this out. "Willow was married once."

Dad frowned. "And now she's divorced, and that bothers you?"

"No, not like that." Austin blew out a frustrated breath. "Willow's husband died awhile back. I believe she said he died of cancer."

"Oh, honey. I'm so sorry." Mom caught his gaze and wouldn't let go. "She's had a great deal of problems."

"Yes, but there's something more. Remember the first day when she came out to check on Jack? She fainted."

"Yes of course. I assumed that she was overly tired."

"No." Austin rose from the couch and paced a few steps. "She fainted because she thought her deceased husband had returned from the dead."

"Returned from the dead?" Mom's mouth dropped open. "Austin, what are you saying?"

Dad folded his arms over his chest. "This whole

conversation is getting weird."

"I know, I know. Here's the bottom line, the entire problem. I look exactly like Willow's husband."

"Have you asked her to show you a picture of him?" Mom said.

"Good idea." Why hadn't he thought of that before?

"If you see an image of this person, you can judge for yourself as well. What else did she say about the similarity?"

"We look the same, even down to a mole that I have on the left side of my neck except, he had one on the right side in the exact spot." Austin touched his neck. "Her husband's interests were the same including some of my boyhood hobbies. Yet, I'm no relation to him whatsoever. It's incredible."

Mom peered out toward the pasture for several moments, as if weighing her next words. Then she turned to Dad and whispered. "I'm not sure why there was someone who looked exactly like Austin, but I think it's time he knew."

Austin scooted in beside his mother. "Time for what, Mom, Dad?"

Under furrowed brows, Dad tightened his lips. "There's something that we never told you."

Mom gripped his hand. "Please listen and try to understand. And Austin, your father and I love you very much. We always have."

Austin stared straight ahead. Only the silhouette

of the rolling hills was still visible. The faint outline of the backyard trees was shrouded against the night sky—shrouded the same way his mother and father had apparently hidden something from him all these years.

Dad began in a quiet voice. "A long time ago, something occurred in our lives, but your mother and I agreed to keep it a secret as best we could."

What now? Austin's heart raced. "Look, I'm twenty-eight years old. I think I'm old enough to understand anything you need to tell me."

"You're right, son. I suppose we were waiting for a time when it was absolutely necessary." Dad said.

"Okay, I'm seriously stressing out now." Austin paced again. "Why wouldn't you want to tell me something?"

Mom took a long breath. "When Tim, Jace and Erica were born, we didn't choose them, though we were more than happy to have them born into our family." Mom chuckled. "Especially Erica. She was our last child, as you know, but we hadn't planned for her birth at all—especially hadn't anticipated having a girl."

"Mom, what are you trying to tell me?" He gripped her hands in his. "What about me?"

Mom lowered her voice as if to soften the impact of what she planned to say. "When you were born, we chose you. Everything about you. You were a precious baby boy with a full head of blond hair. You wanted your bottle every three hours when you first arrived on the ranch, and as you grew, we knew we'd made no mistake in bringing you into our family. You were the sweetest child ever."

Austin peered at the trees in the back pasture again and held his breath for a moment then released it. For more than two minutes words didn't come to him. He knew exactly what his mom was telling him. "You adopted me. Why didn't you tell me before?"

Dad rose from the couch and gave him an easy punch to his shoulder. "You were as much our child as the other three. We never told anyone. Even Tim, Jace, or Erica."

"Yes, but why?"

"We loved you so much from the very start," Mom said. "We didn't want them to think you were any less important to us or as a member of our family. We didn't want to hurt you emotionally or cause feelings of rejection in any way. Who knows how your young brothers may have reacted?"

"But why did you adopt me? It wasn't as if you wanted another child and couldn't have one. After all, Erica was born later."

Dad scratched his head. "It's a long story."

Austin folded his arms over his chest and sat up straight. "I've got all night."

Dad took a seat on Austin's other side. "It just so happened that your mother had been ill for several months before we got you. She didn't come into town much so nobody really noticed whether she was pregnant or not."

"What about my brothers and sister? Didn't they wonder when you brought home a baby?"

"Sweetie, Erica wasn't even born, and Jace and Tim were under two so they didn't think anything about it," Mom reasoned.

"Someone in the community had to have known."

Mom looked at Dad, and he nodded. "Mr. Packard has been a lawyer in our community for years."

"The older guy whose office is downtown? I heard he was planning to retire," Austin said.

"He likely is. But this was almost thirty years ago. One evening, we got a call from a Mrs. Rawlins who was a social worker for the state. She asked if she could come out to the ranch for a visit that night."

Austin's eyes widened as he listened to his mother's voice.

"She said that someone had left a baby boy in the custody of Mr. Packard several weeks before. The mother had received no prenatal care. When she gave birth to a baby boy, he wasn't expected to live because of low birth weight."

What did this have to do with him? Surely, he wasn't the boy. He murmured. "But I did live."

Mom caught his gaze. "Yes, you did."

Dad continued. "The doctor told the mother that you wouldn't live. The biological father had abused her, so she feared for her life. She fled but not before giving

Mr. Packard power of attorney to bury the child."

Mom sighed. "That night, the social worker said she knew our family was one of the most gracious and caring folks in the community. She asked Dad and me to pray about this. She said the child needed a quiet environment rather than the hustle bustle of the hospital. She asked if we could care of you until—"

"Until I died."

Mom reached for his hand. "But God saw to it that you didn't. You thrived, and eventually, we adopted you."

Austin froze, unable to move. That little baby, that was him. And he hadn't been expected to live. He hunched over, afraid to look into Dad's eyes. His life would be forever changed now. He wanted to deny what he'd heard, yet he couldn't. Finally, he found the effort to look up. He lifted his hands in the air. "I didn't die. I'm blessed to have good health."

"That's right, son. The doctor said because you had an early diagnosis and treatment, you became healthy." Dad winked at Mom. "We've always attributed this to the Lord. Now you've grown into an active, strong young man."

Mom snuggled next to Austin on the other side and ran her hand over his. "Honey, I know this a lot to take in right now. As you grew into adulthood, Dad and I always considered telling you, but we wanted to keep you from having to digest all of these facts. Can you forgive us?"

Forgive them? The Fords had taken him in and given him a normal life with a family who cared for him. They even taught him about the Lord. Tears filled his eyes as he reached both his arms to draw Mom and Dad closer. "You're right. This will take a long time to digest, but right now, I can only say thank you. Without your care and love, I might not have lived. I love you both."

~

Along the wall closest to the door, a shelf was filled with bags and cans of specialty and organic food options for cats, dogs, and birds. Shampoos, brushes, and nail clippers for pets occupied another display.

Willow had to admit, the store was impressively well-stocked. "I appreciate this opportunity to work at your store." She smiled at the owner.

Mr. Roi shook her hand. "Doctor Lawson, I'm happy to have you as an employee. It's not every day that I can hire a veterinarian. I can pay you a little more because of your qualifications, but certainly not what you deserve."

Willow's pulse picked up speed. "I had an idea. What would you think of an after-hours educational clinic to be held here at the store? Perhaps a workshop on how to best support your horse's health or caring for a cat in your home. I certainly wouldn't charge you for this. It could attract new customers to your store."

A broad smile covered his face. "I think that's a great idea. We can talk about it in a few weeks."

"I want to give back to the community in some way."

"Can you start tomorrow afternoon for the second shift?"

"For sure." *Thank You, Lord.* This job would see her through financially while waiting to settle with the insurance company.

Willow turned toward her apartment two streets from the pet store. Since Oakville Pet and Feed was so close, she could walk.

She inhaled the evening air, fragrant with cedar and mesquite, as a warm breeze offered a welcome relief from the day's heat.

She turned onto her walkway to the ground-floor apartment and unlocked the door. The central air cooled her face and arms.

The day she discovered the break-in came rushing back, sending a chill down her spine. Thank the Lord she hadn't boarded a patient at the time. Though she regretted not operating her clinic now, at least she could still make ranch and house calls.

Willow walked into the kitchen and opened the refrigerator door for a bottle of water. She unscrewed the cap and strolled to the back window.

In the backyard, a shadow shifted and disappeared behind the side of the building.

A chill of fear raced down her spine. Someone

was out there, but did she want to check? She mustered her courage and slipped out the back door.

Peeking around the side of the apartment, she stood still, paralyzed, afraid someone would be there, but no, she saw no one. Her imagination tricked her?

She turned and crept inside, locking the door behind her. What would anyone want from her? She had nothing of value in her apartment, especially now that her equipment had been destroyed.

Her mother-in-law or the Ford family certainly wouldn't want to harm her. Then who? Was it one of the intruders who'd threatened her? She sighed. Perhaps she'd only imagined she saw someone in the backyard.

Chapter Ten

Willow parked in front of the Whitlock ranch house and stepped out of the van. In the backseat, a bucket filled with cleaning supplies, her vacuum, and a stack of dirty rags waited to be unloaded later at home. Today, her heart swelled with satisfaction. Cleaning Emma's house earlier had brought a deep sense of fulfillment, and the gratitude shining in Emma's eyes was the only reward she needed.

Mr. Whitlock walked out the front door of his single-story dwelling. "Good morning, Dr Lawson. Nice to see you today. Thanks for coming out to check on Ranger."

She pulled her ponytail through her ball cap. "Yes, sir. I'm on my way to visit a patient at the Fords' ranch later, so this worked out fine. How's my friend Ranger doing? Behaving himself?"

Mr. Whitlock stood, shifting from side to side. "I made sure he don't get loose. No point in him exploring the pasture or finding his way to the Fords' property again. Only causes trouble."

She nodded, determined to say no more.

Mr. Whitlock led Willow around the house and to the barn out back. "He's right in here."

Ranger lay on his dog bed inside a fenced enclosure.

"Hey, Ranger. How ya doing today?" Willow entered into the little wire fence and knelt down next to the border collie.

The thump, thump of his tail pleased her.

She examined Ranger for swelling around the cast. She gently moved his leg, and, thankfully, he didn't wince. "I think he's gonna be fine in a couple more weeks. Continue to keep him isolated for now, and I'll check on him next week."

Mr. Whitlock chewed a piece of hay. "Dr Lawson, this town needs you. I hope you can get your clinic up and running before too long."

Willow smiled. "You're not the only one. As soon as I settle with the insurance company and I'm able to purchase new equipment, I should be in business again."

Mr. Whitlock lowered his voice. "Not to pass on gossip or nothing, but those disturbances over at the Fords' ranch are still going on. I've seen lights over there at least once or twice a week. One time in the middle of the night."

"I'm sure the Fords are as anxious to get to the

bottom of this as you are." Willow rubbed her hand along Ranger's furry head one more time and stood. "I'll be back in a few more days."

"Think ya, Dr Lawson. In the meantime, Ranger ain't steppin' off this property."

Willow made the short drive to the Fords' ranch, only a half mile down the road. She turned in at the sign and drove up the road, stopping at the horse barn. Austin would be there in a minute or two, she was sure.

Inside, she proceeded to Jack's stall. "Hey, buddy, you're looking better today."

Jack's coat appeared a little shinier and some of the gleam had reappeared to his eyes.

"You eatin good? Guess those oats are tasting a little better these days."

Footsteps echoed behind her near the barn door. A shadow appeared, and a hoarse voice spoke. "Is there something you want? What are you doing on the Ford property?" A thirty something man with a scruffy beard marched toward her.

Willow caught her breath and yelped. "Who, who are you?"

"I might ask you the same thing. The Fords have had a lot of disturbances on this ranch and can't be too careful. Does the owner know why you're here?"

Willow swallowed hard. "No. I should've called ahead but—"

The man stared her down. "If no one knew you

were coming, I'd say we have a problem." He looked at her with a furious frown.

"Hey, Jace, what's going on in here?"

Willow let out a breath of relief. She pointed to Austin. "He knows me."

"Oh, hey bro. I saw this person come into the barn. I figured she was one of the diggers you've been telling me and Charlotte about. Sorry, lady."

Austin threw back his head and guffawed. "You didn't notice her van with Lawson Veterinarian Clinic on the side?"

Jace gave a playful punch to his forehead. "Guess not."

"Time for introductions. Willow, allow me to introduce my brother, Jace Ford. He owns and operates his own ranch about ten miles from here. Jace, Doctor Lawson, the veterinarian."

Jace placed a hand over his heart in mock repentance. "Dr. Larson, do forgive me. I came by to drop off a post hole driver I borrowed from my father last fall and saw your van." He chuckled. "Dad mentioned intruders in the back pasture. and I suppose I've been on the lookout." He stuck out his hand.

Willow shook hands with the guy, a towering figure with broad shoulders and a sturdy, muscular build. "No problem. I can understand how you're all on alert here at the ranch."

Jace wiped his brow and turned to leave. "I need to speak with Dad to ask his advice on purchasing a new tractor. Once more, Dr. Lawson, I'm sorry to have mistaken you for an intruder. I'll mind my own business for the rest of the day." He chuckled.

If Willow wasn't mistaken, Jace's cheeks had paled to a light pink.

"See you later, Jace." Austin neared Jack's stall. "I believe our patient is doing a little better today."

"Continue with his antibiotics at least another week, and I'll check on him again. This equine flu is hard to kick for some horses." She stroked Jack's jaw. "Any leads as to who might be digging on your property?"

"Not yet. Dad considered calling the sheriff, but then we haven't had any fresh holes."

Last night's events crept into her thoughts—the shadow she saw or imagined. Or, like the Fords, was someone looking for something or spying on her? "I thought I saw someone outside in my backyard last night."

Austin glanced at her with an expression of concern and wrinkled his brow. He reached for her hand.

"This is a long shot, but since someone was out to destroy my lab and left a warning to go back home, I wonder if the same person showed up last night?"

Austin gripped her hands harder and turned her to face him. "I'm sorry, Willow. I don't want to see you in any kind of danger. Did you call the sheriff?"

"No." She took in a quick breath. The thought

pierced, like a needle's point. "What if the person who destroyed my lab was the same as the diggers on your property?"

Austin tilted his head and frowned. "I don't know. I can't wrap my mind around the notion. There's no real connection between you and the Ford family other than you are our veterinarian."

Willow filled her cheeks with air and blew out. "None of it makes any sense."

Strong arms drew her closer. She melted into the protection of Austin's embrace. "I prayed that nothing will harm you. I care about you, Willow—from the first time you fainted and I held you in my arms."

~

Austin held on, unwilling to release her. He breathed in Willow's scent—like fresh peaches. "What time do you go to work today?"

"Oh, I still have a couple of hours." She murmured.

"I need to take the ATV out to check the north pasture? Wanta go?" If Austin had his way, she'd be by his side for more days than just today.

She stepped back, searching his eyes. "Yes, I'll be happy to."

He leaned closer to her, his pulse taking off. "Every morning when I get up, I pray that there'll be no more signs of the intruders. In fact, if I see anything else today, I'm seriously thinking about going to the sheriff." Austin turned toward the equipment shed. "Let's grab the ATV."

In the radiant daylight, Willow followed him. "Whoever caused this trouble, I hope they've become discouraged and left."

In front of the shed, Austin helped Willow into the vehicle and started the engine. After a fifteen-minute bumpy ride to the location of the previous holes, he glanced about fifty yards in front of him. If he wasn't mistaken, the number of holes seemed to have increased. Arriving at the first opening in the ground which he was certain hadn't been there before, he braked and then gritted his teeth. "This one is deep."

Willow scratched her head. "Do you suppose someone is trying to dig a water well? But why would they do that without your permission?"

Austin gave a frustrated chuckle. "Maybe a group of archeologists are searching for buried artifacts. This entire area used to be in habited by Indian tribes."

Willow gave his arm an easy punch. "Even so, people can't dig on your property without your permission." She pointed to a clump of grass about three feet from her. "Speaking of artifacts, look at that tobacco tin."

Austin took a tentative step forward. A small, circular container rested in the grass. He reached toward the object and picked it up. "Not an artifact, I'm afraid. This is a plain old, everyday tobacco tin."

Willow leaned closer as if examining the object. "Does anyone in your family chew tobacco?"

"No. No one, including Mac, Chet, and Pete."

"Do you think this could be trash that's blown from another location?" Willow brushed a long strand of her dark hair behind her ear. "Or do you think the digger dropped it?"

"I don't know. However, I do know one thing. I've had enough. I'm going to talk to dad, and we're going to figure this out."

Chapter Eleven

The next afternoon, Austin shook hands with the deputy. "I appreciate you coming out today. My father and I both agree on our decision to file a report with your office."

The sheriff crouched down, his brow furrowed as he carefully examined the strange, irregular holes in the ground. "You did the right thing." He glanced toward the other deputy shaking Dad's hand and to the six-foot cavity again. "It appears that one or more people have illegally trespassed on your land, digging on property which doesn't belong to them. No wild animal would make a hole that deep." He scratched his head. "What confuses me is why would someone show up on your ranch like this. What are they looking for? Whatever they think they're going to find must be worth something."

Austin eyed his dad. Could this have anything to do with his great grandfather Jeremiah and the rumors of gold? He couldn't imagine how. After all these years, if there was gold buried on the ranch, wouldn't someone have found the treasure by now?

The first deputy rose from inspecting the hole. "Austin, we'll write up a full report and file it at the office. In the meantime, we'll send patrol cars out this way more frequently. If we catch them, we can give them a trespass warning, and if they come on the property again after that, we can arrest them. I'll send out investigators tomorrow to see if they can determine why someone has this much interest in your ranch."

Austin patted the deputy on the shoulder. "I appreciate it."

The deputy raised his index finger. "I would suggest you begin by securing your various buildings on the ranch. Put alarms on all your storage sheds, barns, and, of course, your home. Make sure that you have adequate lighting around the property."

"Yes, sir. Thanks for the advice." Austin waved to the deputies as they got in their patrol car and drove in the direction of the main road.

Dad approached from behind and stood next to Austin. He filled his cheeks with air and blew it out again. "Those blamed fools …" His face turned purple, and he gripped his chest.

Austin reached for Dad's elbow and maneuvered him toward the ATV. "You need to relax. We're gonna take care of this."

Dad appeared to have aged in the last several

months. Owning and operating a large, Texas sheep ranch no doubt had taken a toll on his father. If his dad would only allow him, he'd take even more responsibility. A move he believed would happen sooner rather than later.

Austin summoned his inner strength to battle the growing anxiety. If Dad wasn't careful, he might have a heart attack. "God is going to see us through and protect our ranch." He saw Dad into the passenger's seat and then drove back to the house.

Dad clenched his fists. "You know, son, a year or so ago, we had some big problems here at the ranch."

"I remember."

"Sales were low, wool production wasn't up to par, and our finances looked bleak."

The ATV bounced and rocked, shaking Austin as they trailed along the dirt road. "About the same time Peyton had that accident and started doing some of the office work for you."

"Yep. We weren't looking good. There was one moment when I actually believed we'd have to sell the ranch—the ranch our family has owned for four generations."

"I didn't realize that things had gotten that bad. I can't imagine selling this property for as long as it's been in our family."

"That's right." Dad took a long breath and exhaled slowly. "I want you to know, son. I can remember the day we gave it up to the Lord. Then

Peyton proved to be an excellent manager and eventually got our ranch out of the red. Finally, we were back on track. If God can do those kinds of miracles, He can see us out of this mess."

A rush of warmth enveloped Austin's chest. His dad's positive attitude was another miracle as far as he was concerned.

After Austin dropped Dad off to take a rest, he parked the ATV in front of the horse barn. Now if he could only see Jack well again.

And learn more about the man Willow Lawson mistook him for the first time she saw him.

~

At the pet store, Willow approached the lady peering at the aquarium filled with a variety of fish. "Is there something I can help you with, ma'am?"

The woman wearing a brown felt Stetson and white eyelet shirt smiled and turned toward Willow, her expression brightening. "I'd like to buy an aquarium and several fish, but I don't know where to start."

To think, Willow's first day at the pet shop and the woman asked her something she could easily answer. "Let's see. The aquarium needs to be large enough to accommodate the number of fish you have. Make sure to use treated water and not tap water." She explained how to keep the water clean, using appropriate light and an infiltration system.

After the customer paid for her purchases, she shook Willow's hand. "Thank you so much. I appreciate your information. You seem so well informed."

Willow chuckled. She wouldn't tell the woman that care of fish, amphibian, and reptiles comprised almost an entire semester in vet school. She returned to the shelf where she stocked specialized dog and cat food. She let out a soft sigh, her shoulders relaxing. If she couldn't run her vet clinic, this was the next best thing.

Mr. Roi, her boss, juggled a load of boxes heading for the stockroom.

Willow leaned slightly forward, raising her brow. "Sir, I have an idea I need to bounce off you."

"Sure, Willow." Mr. Roi continued toward the back of the store. "Let me put these boxes up first."

Not more than three minutes later, her boss returned. "I'm grateful to have a veterinarian working for me in the shop. You're an asset."

"Thank you. That's what I wanted to talk about. The free community workshops I mentioned: what would you think of me focusing on the proper feed for horses and sheep for the first one?"

Mr. Roi nodded, his glistening eyes showing agreement. "Sounds good. The information will be so valuable to the local ranchers."

"And, we can encourage them to purchase their food here." Willow smiled. "I'll get to work on setting up the first session."

Later, Willow glanced at her watch. Her first shift had sailed by. Mr. Roi would be closing shop soon. She grabbed her purse. "See you tomorrow, boss."

She climbed into the van parked on the street in front of the store. Though her apartment was only a few blocks away, she didn't want to risk someone following her home again.

Pulling up in front of her apartment, she turned off the ignition and headed up the sidewalk to her door.

Something that looked like white paper lay on her doorstep. She picked up her pace and walked closer. An object that appeared to be a picture was secured by a rock. She shoved the rock to one side and reached for the photo.

Who would leave a picture on her doorstep? In the dim light, she unlocked the door and stepped inside.

Setting her purse on the table, she glanced at the image, and then her jaw dropped open. She took in a sharp breath of air.

Her fingers tightened around the glossy photo, her gaze fixed on Jesse's face. Her hands shook as she turned the picture over and then sucked in a breath.

We know what you're after. Back off.

The threatening message sent chills down her spine. The photo which had sat on her desk in her lab, a picture of Jesse which had disappeared the day of the break-in, now served as a menacing presence.

No doubt whoever ransacked her lab had stolen it and then left her husband's picture on her doorstep, but why? Someone who wanted to make some kind of statement. Someone who wanted to punish her by reminding her of the tragedy. The sooner she took this evidence to the sheriff, the better.

The photo slipped from her hand, drifting to the floor as Willow covered her eyes. Her shoulders trembled, consumed by sobs that shook her body.

Chapter Twelve

Austin inserted his key in the mailbox at the post office in Oakville and pulled out the handful of letters. He thumbed through the bills and advertisements, tossing some of the ads in the garbage.

The next letter was an envelope with no return address. Walking back to his truck, he set the rest of the mail in the passenger seat and opened the odd-looking letter. He read the type written message: *we are watching your every move. Don't do anything dumb.*

Austin shook his head from one side to the other. Did this letter have any connection to the holes in the backyard? The only option now was to take this to the sheriff. Maybe his department could find a way to identify the writer.

His phone rang, and he answered it.

"Austin, this is Willow. Do you have a moment?"

"Yes, I'm in town right now."

"Good. I don't go to work for a couple more hours. Could you stop by for a few minutes? I have to show you something I found on my doorstep last night." She gave him the address of her apartment.

Willow's voice held the same concern he'd detected when she told him about her husband and how he resembled Austin.

Odd how they both received some sort of correspondence. "I'll be there in five minutes. I have something to show you, too." Austin drove a couple of blocks through town and parked in front of her apartment building. Opening the door of the truck, he got out and trekked up her sidewalk, not sure what she had to show him. Was it something she'd ordered for her clinic—or something of a more menacing nature as her tone indicated?

The door flew open and Willow, in jeans and T shirt, met him at the threshold. No smile on her face, she must've had bad news as well—a similar letter to his.

Austin walked into the modest living room with the kitchen toward the back and a bedroom on the right.

She pointed to the couch, a look of confusion on her face. "Sit down, please. You said you had something to show me. You go first."

Austin sank down on the leather couch, Willow beside him. "I'm planning to drop this off at the sheriff's office as soon as I leave here." He passed the letter to Willow.

Willow took the letter out of the envelope and after a minute, her eyes grew large. She glanced up at him. "What do you think this means?"

"I asked myself the same thing. Is this related to the digging in the back pasture? I have a strange notion it is."

Willow ran her hand down his. "I'm so sorry, Austin. You're doing the right thing reporting it to the sheriff. They're the professionals and can handle the situation."

"Yes. I keep telling myself the same. But who could possibly be watching my every move, and what do they mean by don't do something dumb?"

"Do you suppose they mean don't go to the sheriff? It's ridiculous to tell you not to when you've received a threatening letter."

"I have one more concern." He fixed his gaze on her and held it. "My mom and dad. I pray that they aren't in any danger."

"Prayer is our best option." Willow bowed her head. "Lord, please protect Austin's parents as well as the Ford ranch. Help me to restore my clinic as soon as possible. Amen."

The vision of the lovely woman, eyes closed, speaking to God made him realize how he had someone who cared about him. He wasn't facing this alone. "You said you had something to show me?"

"Yes." Willow reached into her pocket and pulled out what looked like a worn photograph. She passed it to him. "This was on my doorstep last night when I came home from work."

Austin took the photo from her and then raised his eyebrows. It was a picture from Mom's album—one of him a couple of years ago. "Willow, you said someone left this last night? I don't understand. This is me after I graduated from college, but I thought Mom had put all these old photos away in a box she keeps in the closet. She hasn't taken these out in a while."

Willow slowly shook her head, her eyes glassy. "This isn't a picture of you, Austin. It's Jesse. It was taken a few months before he died."

Austin sat with his mouth open. "I don't understand."

Willow gripped his hand. "This picture went missing the day my clinic was ransacked." She turned it over.

Austin read the words scribbled in heavy black ink. "We know what you're after. Back off." He glanced up at her. "That makes no sense."

Willow lifted a sad gaze to his. "I know. I'm afraid I'm up against some kind of hidden foe. How can I fight against an enemy if I have no idea who they are or what they want?"

Austin sat still for a moment and then smoothed his hand over hers. "Unfortunately, I have an idea who may have sent this."

Willow's jaw dropped open. "Are you thinking the same people who sent you the letter today?"

"It could be. They've likely seen you with me and figure you're involved in some way in helping me look for the gold—and they want to frightened you away."

~

The next morning, Willow walked out of the Ford's barn and turned to Austin. "You were right in calling me to check on that ewe."

"The creature's weight loss was evident." Austin closed the barn door after them.

"The sheep likely suffers from a gastrointestinal disease, but I'll know more when I send the samples to the lab. In any case, we've caught it in time. Now she can't pass it on to the other animals." Willow replaced her stethoscope in her bag and headed toward her van.

Austin caught her attention as she opened the door. "It's so strange the way I resemble Jesse. Even I was fooled by the picture you showed me yesterday."

Willow swallowed hard. "I'm as confused as you are. The first day I saw you, I was convinced I'd seen a phantom. How is it that you have a mole in the exact same spot as my husband, but on the opposite side? Your interests are so similar that it's eerie."

Austin swiped his hand down the side of his jeans and cleared his throat. "There's something I haven't told you." He paused a moment, staring over her shoulder. "My mom and dad pulled me aside and said I needed to know the truth, that they regretted waiting so long."

Willow held her breath. The truth about Austin? What did he mean?

"They said they began caring for me when I was about two weeks old and eventually adopted me."

"Austin." Willow widened her eyes and gripped his hand.

"Even now it seems strange to say those words. But they told me how they'd always kept the truth from my siblings as well as the town's people. They said they never wanted me to feel different from my siblings or less loved."

Willow stared at Austin a moment, trying to process what he'd said. Austin adopted? "Do you suppose you and Jesse could be related? Or perhaps even brothers?"

Austin lifted his hands in apparent frustration. "I don't know what to think. Mom didn't tell me who my birthmother was, or whether she had any other children. I don't believe my parents know." He sighed. "But since learning about your husband, I can't help but think that the answer is pointing in that direction."

"Did your mother tell you who handled the adoption?"

"Yes, she said that the local lawyer, Mr. Packard, handled it. I'm going to drop by his office if I can, but I'm not sure what he could tell me."

Then a chill raced her spine. If by some bizarre

turn of events, Austin and Jesse were brothers, then Emma was Austin's mother as well. But she couldn't mention it to Austin now. Not with all the other life altering facts he absorbed recently. Only one thing to do, pay a visit to Emma tonight after work. "I guess I better head to the pet shop."

Austin frowned. "You came to Oakville in good faith and started your business here. I'm sorry that everything has worked against you. Now the Ford family is coping with a web of challenges that feel overwhelming." He drew her to him and held her tight.

For a few seconds, Willow basked in his arms. Then she backed away. If she closed her eyes and drank in Austin's scent, she was in Jesse's arms again.

~

Willow knocked on Emma's door and then held her breath. In only moments, Willow could possibly know the truth—truth that her mother-in-law may have held from her.

The door squeaked open. "Willow, this is a surprise." Her mother-in-law smiled and opened the door wider. "Please come in."

Willow wandered into the modest living room and glanced around. Several pictures adorned the small hearth, with one more on the side table beside Emma's recliner. Most were of Jesse, except for the one by the chair, which featured both her and Jesse together.

Emma pointed to the couch. "Would you like some tea, dear?"

Willow nodded. The very thing she needed. "Chamomile, if you have it."

"Of course." Emma moved with a slow, labored gait, each step appearing to require considerable effort.

How could this dear woman not tell her the truth? Emma had always treated her with kindness and was willing to help, to act as a second mother. If Jesse's dear mother had answers for her tonight, she'd believe what she said.

After a few minutes, Emma returned with a delicate, hand-painted cup of steaming tea. The aroma of apples, fresh-cut hay, and honey filled the air. Setting the cup down on the coffee table, she retrieved her own from the kitchen and relaxed adjacent to Willow.

Emma smiled. "I appreciate you coming to see me." She pointed to her legs. "I don't get out very much to visit with my neighbors."

"I know you don't, and I'm sorry."

"Don't be, dear. I know how busy you are with your job and getting your clinic back in order. Plus, you've been so kind as to clean my house."

Willow swallowed hard. Emma could disclose life changing facts in only moments. She couldn't put it off any longer. "Emma." She attempted to steady her breath. "I need to ask a question, and you may wonder why I ask. Fair warning, it's quite personal, even profound. I will understand if you don't want to answer."

Emma frowned. "Dear, I can't imagine what you plan to ask, but I would never keep anything from you. You're the only family I have left in this world."

Willow rubbed her damp hands together. "When Jesse was born, did you have a second baby, his twin?"

Emma met Willow's gaze and touched her hand. "No, Willow. I've only had one child—Jesse, your deceased husband."

Chapter Thirteen

For the past week, Austin had tried to piece the puzzle together. But no matter how hard he tried, nothing seemed to fit—every clue felt like a dead end. He shoveled manure out of Jack's stall and sprayed the area with bleach.

For what felt like the hundredth time, he went over the facts. Willow's late husband had looked uncannily like him, sharing the same traits and habits. And then there was the undeniable truth—Austin was adopted. Mom and Dad knew nothing about the birth parents and weren't sure if Mr. Packard could give them information.

Austin laid fresh wood shavings on the floor and gave Jack a pat. Another consideration: Jesse lived in California all his life, and Austin lived in central Texas.

He shrugged and glanced at Jack. "Hey, buddy. Looks like you're feeling better. I think I can take you out for a ride pretty soon. I guess I better check with the pretty doctor who comes to see you."

Jack snorted and bobbed his head up and down.

"Give me a break. You didn't just understand what I said." Austin guffawed.

"Austin, I thought I saw you come in here a while ago."

Austin turned to his father's voice behind him. "Mom's having a family dinner tonight and wants to make sure you will be there."

"Sure. What's the occasion?"

Dad took a few steps closer. "Your mom and I decided it's about time we tell your siblings the story of how you came into our family."

Sweat broke out on Austin's brow. Would this news change Austin's relationship with them? "Do you think it's a good idea?"

Dad patted his shoulder. "Look, son. Nothing has changed. You're still a Ford and always will be."

The news offered a sense of reassurance, but only halfway. "Okay. Who's she inviting?"

"Jace and Charlotte and Erica and Peyton. Tim will join us on zoom."

Though he tried to remain positive, he didn't particularly like the idea of a family dinner and a big announcement, especially about him. "Can't we just send everybody a text?"

Dad grinned. "I think that's a good idea, but you know your mother. She's always making a big deal over everything. And Mac said he's going into town for dinner."

Austin poked around Jack's stall for a while and then straightened up the tool shed. He inspected the equipment for needed repairs and watered the garden to the side of the main house. Finally, he couldn't put it off any longer. Almost time for dinner, and his siblings would no doubt each react to the news. Jace might feel betrayed because he was never told. And then Austin could count on his sister to get all teary eyed and emotional. She'd accept him no matter what.

Austin headed to his room and the shower. Toweling off, he glanced in the mirror. Might as well look like a well-groomed adopted brother. He ran the razor over his cheeks and then gave himself a kick in the pants.

He'd only been focused on himself this whole time. He should've thought about how this affected everyone else.

Walking down the steps to the living room, he waved at his sister and her husband coming in the front door.

Erica ran toward him giving him a fierce hug. "Hey brother, I haven't seen you in so long. We left our little girl with Peyton's dad tonight so we can visit with all you guys. I'm so glad Mom decided to have a family dinner."

"Hi, sis." He hugged her back.

Peyton slapped him on his shoulder. "Hey dude, good to see you again."

Austin wanted with all his heart to pretend everything was normal. But he knew it wasn't. "How's the ranch going?"

"We've got six residents now, and dad's shouldering a lot of the work." Peyton smiled. "Sure good to see you again."

Jace helped his shapely wife who must've lost at least fifty pounds out of the truck.

Austin guessed everybody was here now except Tim.

After all the hugs subsided, Mom herded everyone into the living room. "Tim texted. He's caught up in a meeting. We'll talk to him on Zoom later in the evening. But for now, we have an important reason for our family dinner tonight." She glanced at everyone, now seated in the living room. "There's a family issue your father and I have never told any of you except for Austin."

Austin squirmed on the couch where he sat by Erica. The way Mom set up her big announcement sounded like someone was dying or something. He hiked one foot over his knee and then switched sides.

Mom folded her hands and glanced at everyone. "You see. Austin came into our family in a different way than Erica, Jace, and Tim."

Erica frowned. "Mom, what are you trying to say?"

"You see, twenty-eight years ago, we received a call from the social worker who knew our family loved children. At that time, Erica, you weren't born. Only Jace and Tim. Jace was a baby and Tim a toddler."

Jace scratched his head. "Are you saying what I think you're saying?"

Mom continued to tell the same story she and Dad had told him.

Austin studied his boots resting on the floor as first Erica and then Jace stared at him and then back to Mom.

Austin's stomach churned, and he stood. "What Mom is trying to say is I'm adopted. She and Dad's reasons for doing so were unselfish and kind." He glanced at his parents. "And I want to thank you. Mom and Dad thought only of me. They didn't want me to feel any different than the rest of you. They only wanted me to consider myself a part of our family." He walked toward his mother and squeezed her hand. "Mom, I can't thank you enough for that. I've always felt a I belonged to this family—whether by adoption or by birth."

Austin surprised himself. He hadn't expected to become emotional tonight. But since now was a good opportunity to show his gratitude to his parents in front of his siblings, he'd take advantage of the chance. He gave Dad a bear hug. "Thank you for giving me your name and calling me your own."

Erica rose from her place on the couch, tears rolling down her cheeks, and embraced him. "You are now and always will be my brother, and I love you."

What Austin figured would be embarrassing wasn't at all. He gulped hard, fighting to hold his emotions under control. Now, the entire family surrounded him, wrapping him in hugs.

Charlotte gave him a high-five. "No matter what I'm still your sister-in-law, and I love you, Austin."

Jace grinned and pointed to Charlotte. "Yeah, what she said." His face turned a bright red. No doubt he felt more embarrassment than any of them.

After the hugs dwindled, Mom directed them into the dining room. "Tonight, we're having your favorite, Austin. Roast beef with potatoes, carrots, and green beans from the garden and, of course, lemon pie for dessert."

Austin took his place at the table. Though he'd dreaded this family dinner, he never felt more like a Ford. Now the need to uncover his origins was urgent, if only to solve the mystery of how he resembled Willow's late husband.

Monday, he'd call on Mr. Packard to discover what the man knew or could tell him. After all, the lawyer was the only person besides the social worker to have met his biological mother.

~

After breakfast the next morning, Austin gathered the plates from the table, took them to the kitchen, and scraped the bits of scrambled eggs and bacon down the disposal.

With Betsy not here today, Mom stood at the sink filling the dishwasher.

Austin placed his arm around her waist and hugged. "Thanks for being the best mom ever. I'm sure that dinner last night wasn't the easiest for you."

She turned to him. "Sweetie, no doubt it wasn't the easiest for you, either. Your father and I have debated for years whether keeping your adoption a secret all this time was a good idea or not. I suppose the Lord gave us our answer recently. The truth needed to be told, but at this point, only our family members will be privileged to the information."

"And Willow." Austin wiped down the kitchen counter. "When I found out her deceased husband looked exactly like me, I began to wonder and spoke to her about it."

"That's fine." Mom wiped her hands on her apron and gripped Austin's hand. "The day Mr. Packard asked your father and I if we wanted to take care of a precious, very ill little baby boy, he didn't give us a lot of information about you."

A thought loomed in his mind, heavy and unavoidable. "What about a birth certificate?"

"We have your legal birth certificate with your father and I listed as your parents. It states the day you were born, where you were born, your gender, and birth weight and length—the same as that of the rest of our kids."

"What about the original birth certificate?"

"If I'm not mistaken, that one was sealed by the state when we got yours."

Sealed by the state? Would he be able to get a copy of it? "I'd like to pay Mr. Packard a visit, if you don't mind. To see if there's any other information I can find out."

Mom hugged him. "Of course, dear. I can understand why you'd want to. I only wish I could tell you more."

Austin fished out his truck keys from his pocket. "I love you, Mom."

Only one chore to finish and then he'd be on his way to town. He needed to buy feed anyway.

~

Austin stood to his full height, mustering the courage to walk into Mr. Packard's downtown office on Main Street. He opened the door to the old building, which had likely existed since Oakville first received its charter, its weathered facade telling stories of the past. He'd asked himself at least twenty-five times if he was doing the right thing.

In the front office, an elderly woman sat at a desk. She glanced up from her computer. "Yes, sir. How can I help you?"

"I called earlier, and Mr. Packard said he could see me before lunch."

She pointed to an adjacent door toward the back of her office. "He's waiting for you, I believe."

The gray-haired man rose from his desk to shake hands. "Hello, son. Nice to see you. As you can tell, I'm not too busy these days. I'm planning on retiring at the end of this year."

Austin stuck out his hand. "Congratulations, sir."

Mr. Packard chuckled. "It's about time, I'd say. I'll be seventy-five in February."

"You're blessed to have had a long career."

"That's right." Mr. Packard glanced behind Austin. "Mind closing the door?" He relaxed into an office chair and pointed to another across from his desk. "Sit down. I've always figured I'd hear from you one day."

Austin frowned. What did he mean by that? "Then you likely know why I'm here."

He rubbed his forehead. "I do. I've been serving this community for fifty years, and I'm happy to assist you in any way I can."

"The same profession for all this time. I respect that."

"Thank you. How can I help?"

Austin shifted on the chair a couple of times. This was harder than he thought. "You see, sir, my parents recently told me the circumstances around my birth."

Mr. Packard scratched behind his ear. "When

you were born, the Fords wanted to keep the adoption a secret. I suppose that has changed."

"Yes. Mom and Dad only recently told me and my siblings about my adoption. We're not planning to make this public knowledge yet."

"All right." Mr. Packard sat up straight in his chair. "May I ask what has brought about this change?"

"The new veterinarian in Oakview is Dr. Willow Lawson. The first time she saw me, she literally fainted. She thought I was her late husband."

Mr. Packard chuckled. "Returned from the dead?"

"Something like that. I recently spoke with my parents about Willow's husband who looked exactly like me. That prompted them to tell me about my birth. They don't have much information, but now I can't help but wonder if somehow, I'm related to this Jesse Lawson."

Mr. Packard raised a brow and rubbed his chin. "I see."

"In the past month, Willow and I have become—uh, well, more than friends. I suppose you can understand how this would impact our relationship."

Mr. Packard rose from his desk and relaxed into a chair beside Austin's. "I handled the adoption for your parents, and the birth mother requested that her identity wouldn't be revealed."

"Why?"

"Honestly, I believe she was ashamed of her situation and didn't want anyone to know about her choices she later regretted."

Austin steepled his fingers under his chin. "Then you've met her?"

He lowered his voice. "Yes."

Austin's heart pounded out of his chest. "Is there anything you can tell me?"

"Yes. Your birth mother was a lovely young woman. After she gave birth, the doctor told her you would only live a few weeks. She feared your birth father and felt the need to leave as soon as possible. She gave me power of attorney to handle her affairs. She had no idea you actually lived."

A similar story Mom had told him. "What about my birth certificate? My mother said it was sealed by the state."

He nodded. "She's correct. Listen, Austin. Your parents, Mr. and Mrs. Ford, are well known in the community. They are respected as God-fearing Christian people. Child services couldn't have placed you with better folks."

"Isn't there anything else you could tell me?" Austin's face burned. "Was I the only baby? I mean, did I have a twin?"

"The only other thing I can reveal to you is that your mother was in good health."

"Yes, but she was told I wouldn't live."

Mr. Packard twiddled his thumbs. He obviously

knew plenty that he couldn't tell Austin. "If I were to guess, I'd predict you'll get the answers you seek, but they can't come from me. I'm sorry, son."

Austin stood and shook Mr. Packard's hand. "I appreciate your time. I wouldn't want to ask you to speak about a case when you can't. Thank you." Austin returned to his truck and got in. He had little more information than before.

He rested his head on the steering wheel and breathed deeply. If he and Willow were to have a future together, they'd have to be content with what they know now.

But would the lack of information matter to Willow? Would she want to continue in a relationship with him, or would she decide she couldn't love someone who constantly reminded her of her deceased husband? Only time would tell.

Chapter Fourteen

Willow glanced around the conference room to the rear of the pet shop. Taking her mind off of what Emma had told her proved more difficult than she'd thought.

Even after having an entire weekend to mull over her mother-in-law's statement, Willow remained confused. Face it. She didn't have enough information other than Emma's words to draw an intelligent conclusion. If Willow knew the truth, it could impact her life. Emma was probably aware of that, so why would her mother-in-law deceive her about something so important?

Her gaze returned to the audience gathered to hear her presentation.

Mr. Roi scratched his head. "I might have to turn folks away if anyone else shows up. I don't have any more folding chairs."

Willow couldn't help but smile. "Looks like our

first community outreach could be a success."

Mr. Roi glanced at his watch. "It's seven o'clock. Go ahead and start." He gave her a thumbs-up. "This was a great idea, Willow. You can tell folks that the store will be open for thirty minutes after the end of your presentation."

Willow headed to the front of the room and smiled. "Welcome. I'm Willow Lawson. I'm a trained veterinarian, but I'm working for Mr. Roi until I get my clinic set up again."

Mr. Whitlock, in the second row, removed his hat. "We were so sorry to hear what happened. I can vouch for Dr. Lawson. She took great care of my dog, Ranger."

"Thank you, Mr. Whitlock." Willow looked out over the group of people who'd gathered in the conference room—many local ranchers, no doubt.

"Tonight, I'll be focusing on information about feeding your sheep and horses. I realized many of you have run ranches and cared for your animals for years. I hope to share with you some of the latest findings."

A surge of excitement raced her heart. This was her territory, and she thrived on the information. "As you know, horses spend most of their day eating. The amount of food they need can be calculated by their weight. For example, a one-thousand-pound horse will eat approximately sixteen pounds of food per day. So, they generally eat one point six percent of their weight per day."

A man in the back row pulled his black hat with a wide rim farther down over his head. Black curly hair hung around his ears and neck. He waved his hand in the air. "Hey."

"I was planning to take questions later, but go ahead if you prefer."

He pulled on his scruffy beard. "I've got lots of experience on ranches. Just asking this question in case some of these other blockheads around here may want to know. Can I feed my horse ice cream?"

Willow's stomach churned with frustration, a tight knot of anger coiling within her. If anything, he was the blockhead. "No. Horses don't have the digestive enzymes to break down the lactose. The best food for a horse is pasture grass that they can graze. Horses can also eat oats and small amounts of corn, but too much causes problems such as colic, dental problems, and ulcers."

The curly-headed guy scooted down farther in his seat.

Willow's skin tingled. Who was this man? She hadn't seen him before. "I need to add that horses require fresh water, salt, and sometimes supplements to ensure they receive all the necessary vitamins and minerals."

Austin walked in through the door and sat in the front seat. He mouthed his words. "Sorry I'm late."

Though her imagination might have run away with her, Austin's presence brought relief. Later, she could point out the stranger to him and see what he knew about the rough-looking cowboy. And tell Austin about the ridiculous question the guy asked.

"You can also feed your horses concentrates made up of a mixture of things like grains, flaxseed, beet pulp, molasses for energy and flavor, bran, vitamins and minerals, and other ingredients."

Curly Head scowled and raised his hand again. "I never hear tell of giving a horse molasses. Molasses is for pancakes." He roared.

Willow firmed her lips. Looked like this man was only here to disrupt her presentation. "Can we please keep interruptions to a minimum? Your cooperation helps everyone stay focused."

Mr. Roi rose from his seat on the front row toward the door to the conference room. "Unless you want to conduct yourself in a courteous manner, I'd suggest you leave."

The man rolled his eyes and stomped out of the room.

Willow shook her head and smiled at the audience. "I'm sorry. I'm not sure what that was all about, but I wanted to let you know how proud I am to be here in your community."

After thirty more minutes, Willow wrapped up with the last of her talk. "To let you know, while I'm reestablishing my veterinarian clinic, I'm available for ranch and house calls. Thank you, and please look around the store on your way out. We are open for thirty more minutes."

A middle-aged man approached and held out his hand. "Willow, nice to see you again. I'm Peyton Langley's father."

"Yes, same here, Mr. Langley." Willow shook his hand. "I hope you were able to gain a bit of information tonight. I'm sorry about the disruption."

Austin arrived and stood next to her.

"Anytime I can help you out with your animals, please call," she told Mr. Langley.

"Yes, ma'am." The nice-looking, middle aged man with salt and pepper hair turned to walk into the retail section of the store.

Austin folded a couple of chairs and rested them against the wall. "I've never seen that cowboy around here before. I hope he didn't leave you with a negative opinion of our ranching community."

She shook her head. "I don't believe he represents the other hardworking ranchers in the area." Willow folded a few more chairs and stacked them next to Austin's.

"Mom and Dad said they were sorry not to be here, but Dad was exhausted today."

"I understand." She combed her fingers through her hair. Had tonight's community outreach been successful?

Mr. Roi returned to the conference room. "Thank you, Willow. And we made quite a few sales tonight, as well."

The question burned like the midday, summer sun. "Mr. Roi, do you know who that rude man was?"

Willow's boss continued folding chairs. "No. I've never seen him around here before."

Finally, the seats replaced in the storage cabinet, Willow gathered her purse and made her way to the store's front door.

Austin approached. "Let me see you home."

"Thanks, I'd like that. I have to admit, the presence of that mouthy guy was a bit unsettling. There was something about him …" An uninvited chill ran down her spine.

~

The man glared at the other man. "I can't believe that moron told you to leave."

"Maybe if you would've helped me figure out what to say beforehand …"

The man gave the other man a shove. "At least I'm trying to stay with the plan. What are you doing?"

"Hey. I'm getting a little tired of all of this. Maybe we should move on."

The man grabbed the other man's dirty t-shirt and shook him. "You're in too deep now. Don't even think of it."

Chapter Fifteen

Willow juggled the bags of groceries and hauled them into Emma's house. Inside, she placed the milk, eggs, cheese, and a package of chicken in the refrigerator. The canned goods and loaf of bread went into the cabinet.

Emma, her eyes bright and a wide smile on her face, limped toward her and pointed to the overstuffed easy chair in the living room. "Thank you so much, for the groceries. Let me fix you a cool lemonade." She leaned on her cane as she hobbled toward the kitchen counter.

"Sounds wonderful." Willow slipped into a chair and relaxed her shoulders. Deep down, there might always be the question of whether Emma had told her the truth about Jesse—that she'd never born another. But how could she not trust the dear woman who'd been there to listen to her concerns? Who'd never failed to keep a promise.

Emma returned with a tall, frosted glass with an orange slice perched on the side. She set the drink on the table beside Willow and returned with one for herself.

"Perfect for a summer day. Thanks." Willow sipped the icy liquid and sighed.

Emma sat back in her chair across from Willow. "So, my dear, I forgot to ask the last time we talked, why did you decide to settle in Oakville?"

The sweet, herbal aroma of lavender lingering in the air soothed Willow as she breathed in a long breath. "When Jesse passed away and you left, I was lost, as if riding the California waves with no bearings. I needed to be in the town where Jesse was born. Where you were, even if I was afraid that it would hurt too much to see you again."

Emma reached to squeeze Willow's hand. "You're my family, and I love you."

Willow searched for the courage to ask the question that weighed on her mind. When Jesse was alive, she hadn't felt a need to know, but now, with Austin and Jesse's similarities, the time had come to ask. "Please forgive me if you can't share the answer, but Jesse always said he didn't know who his father was. Do you mind if I ask now?"

Emma twisted her fingers in her lap. The weight of unspoken words hung in the air. Finally, she lifted her head. "I would never take anything for my precious Jesse, but the circumstances around the way he arrived in the world was something I'm not proud of."

Willow leaned forward and gave Emma a soft touch on her shoulder. "We all make mistakes. I can't count the number in my own life. It's one reason I'm grateful for my Savior's forgiveness."

With a slight smile and a nod, Emma met Willow's gaze. "You see, Jesse's father and I were never married. He was a cowboy with a propensity for not staying anywhere very long. He left Oakville after he found out I was pregnant but sent threatening letters."

"What kind of letters?"

"He always had an unhealthy interest in the rumors about one of the Ford ancestors burying gold on the land. The only reason he stayed in town until I got pregnant was to find out what he could about the gold." Emma's voice hitched. "He wrote and said if I didn't tell him about the rumors revolving around the Ford Ranch, he'd harm the baby."

Willow gasped. "That's horrible, Emma."

"So, I packed up Jesse and fled to a small town in California where I thought he'd never find me. And he didn't."

Willow's mouth hung open, and then she snapped it shut. "What a weight to have hanging over you."

Jesse's mother patted her hand. "Don't fret, dear. That was years ago, and I've never heard from the man. I wouldn't be surprised if he'd passed from this earth by now. He's never acted on any of his threats."

The question lingered on Willow's tongue, heavy with unspoken implications. Finally, she mustered the courage to ask. "What did you tell him about the rumors?"

Emma took a slow drink of lemonade. "I was born and raised in Oakville. Jesse's father knew I was aware of the history in this area. I told him all I'd heard."

"Go on."

"The grapevine had it that the original owner of the ranch buried treasure, possibly gold coins, somewhere on the property and never unearthed them." Emma's face turned a soft shade of pink. "Jesse's father had come to Oakville after hearing the tale. He used me to gain information and he—" She covered her face with her hands.

Willow stood to give her a hug. "Please don't relive anymore of the past. I can see how painful it is for you."

"Yes, but I regret my what I did."

"Emma, you were an innocent young woman. The man took advantage of you."

Emma looked up, eyes filled with tears. "I can only thank Jesus for His forgiveness and acceptance of me in His kingdom."

Willow whispered. "You did a wonderful job of raising Jesse on your own. Did you know he taught me about the Lord and how to be a Christian?"

"God used Jesse to spread the gospel to you, like yeast expands through dough." Emma relaxed into her chair. "I'll never regret teaching him about God." She sighed. "But there is something else."

Willow frowned. "What is it?"

Emma opened her mouth to speak, sucked in a breath, and exhaled. She clasped a hand over her mouth. "Forgive me, my child. I want you to tell you, but I, er, I can't now. I'm not ready yet."

~

Austin glanced at Willow, her ponytail flowing from the opening in the back of her ballcap.

She reached toward Jack and hugged his neck.

Austin averted his gaze. What was his problem? Not just the ballcap and ponytail, but the vision of her curves had drawn his attention and traveled beyond the surface of his thoughts. He shouldn't think of her that way. At least not yet. Not until he knew her better—and more of the circumstances around her life.

Willow stroked Jack's mane and smiled. "Okay, fella. I officially declare you well. No more flu for you." She looked over her shoulder at Austin. "Is he eating well now?"

"Yeah. Since a couple of days ago. I can't keep his trough full. It's like he's making up for all those meals he missed."

She gave Jack one more pat and gathered her

equipment. "Thank you for seeing me home the other night after my presentation." She took a few steps toward him.

He chuckled. "I'm glad the sight of me does make you faint these days—like when we first met."

She cast her gaze to the fresh straw in Jack's stall. "I'm sorry about that day."

He touched her shoulder. "Look, I understand. Your patient's owner looks exactly like your deceased husband." He ran a quick hand through his hair. "I only wish we could find out what's going on."

"Me, too." She turned to face him. "Austin, I …"

Austin didn't know too much about women, but if he could guess, Willow needed a hug. Or maybe more. He drew her against his chest, ran his hand down her long hair, and whispered. "I want to protect you from that jerk at the outreach and whoever destroyed your clinic. I want to be there for you."

He caught his breath as she nestled closer, the feel of her delicate skin sending his heart racing.

"I could remain here forever. I'm so grateful to have you as a friend." She tightened her hold around his neck.

A friend? He had to admit the truth. He wanted more than friendship.

Then he stiffened and took a step away combing his fingers through his hair.

Pain radiated from Willow's eyes. "What is it?"

"Maybe we're rushing things. Maybe I should figure out my life first." He caught his breath. "Maybe it's too soon for you since Jesse—" The thought nearly choked him. He was fully ready for a relationship with her, but was he a stand-in for Jesse? The notion flashed a bright red warning in his heart.

Chapter Sixteen

Austin filed the last tooth of the chainsaw and returned the tool to its place on the shelf. He rolled the wheelbarrow to the middle of the room to repair the front wheel.

Dad tapped and entered the tool shed. "Hey, son. Could you come up to the office? There's someone who wants to apply for a job as a ranch hand."

Austin parked the wheelbarrow against the wall and headed for the door. "Sure, but I didn't know you were looking to hire."

"I wasn't. This guy showed up in an old Chevy truck and said he'd seen an ad in Ranch Life Daily."

Austin walked by Dad's side toward the main house. "You did put an ad in a year ago for parttime help before Chet took the job. This guy must've read an old copy."

"True. I figured I might as well hear him out. We could use one more ranch hand next spring during lambing, but that's almost a year away." Dad gestured to a cowboy sitting in the driver's seat of a rusty truck parked by the side of the house. "Maybe we can get his contact information for a future date."

Austin raised an eyebrow.

The dude looked as if he could use a job with his well-worn jeans and boots. A long-handled mustache grew over his upper lip, and a well-used Stetson with frayed edges and a discolored brim sat on his head.

Dad led him into the office by the side door. "Sit down." He pointed to a chair in front of his desk. "This is my son Austin who'll help with the interview."

Austin's chest swelled. His father had begun to depend more on him these days—especially since Jace and Erica had moved.

"I didn't catch your name?" Dad took a seat behind his desk, sitting up straight and looking very official.

"Er, Tex Brown. I'm from Las Lunas, up in the Panhandle. I worked for the Triple Sixes Ranch up there. The only reason I got laid off was because the ranch went out of business."

Austin sniffed, trying not to take in the stale odor emanating from Tex. "Do you have any papers of recommendation?"

The middle-aged cowboy pulled his hat down further on his brow and shook his head. "Naw. The ranch went under too fast, and I weren't able to get none."

The guy's unkept hair appeared as if he hadn't washed it in several weeks—or taken a shower.

An idea began to take shape, and Austin pulled out his cell phone. He typed in Triple Sixes Ranch, Texas Panhandle. Nothing came up. He glanced at Dad and then typed in Las Lunas, Texas. Again nothing.

Austin cleared his throat and stood. "Dad, I recommend we talk about this for a while."

Dad nodded. "Yep. Do you have a phone number where we can get ahold of you."

Tex's upper lip curled, and he shook his head. "Naw. I figured a fancy outfit like yours wouldn't want to hire me, anyway. You uppity people are too good to help me out." He rose and stomped toward the door.

The outline of a round tobacco tin in Tex's back pocket caught Austin's attention. After he shut the door with a bang, Austin held his cell phone up so Dad could see the screen. "That guy was a phony. There's no such town as Las Lunas in the Texas Panhandle nor was there a Triple Sixes Ranch."

~

Austin squinted and shaded his brow with his hand cupped over his eyes. The rundown truck puttered and groaned, the rusty tailgate swaying from the years. The bedraggled cowboy took a right onto the main road.

The man's unkept appearance, thin frame, and lack of personal hygiene, all clued Austin in. The guy had a rough life and was likely broke. For a moment, sympathy engulfed him. He hated to see any human living in such difficult circumstances. But to come to the ranch and lie after he and Dad, in good faith, invited him in—well, Austin wouldn't tolerate it.

Austin set out for the tool shed. The wheelbarrow waited for a repair—as well as some of the other equipment.

Finishing up the wheel repair, he organized the garden tools on the shelf near the door. In the corner, an instrument with a long shaft and a coil on the end was propped up in the corner. *Hmm.* He grasped hold of the implement. A metal detector that Dad had used a couple of years ago to locate property markers and pins ignited an idea in his brain.

He set the instrument in the ATV and headed to the north pasture. Why hadn't he thought of this before? If intruders trespassed upon their land and searched for Great Grandfather's gold, he could do the same.

The afternoon sun blazed, its heat radiating against Austin's skin. After an hour of searching, he wiped his brow. Using the metal detector was hard work and frustrating, and he could no longer adjust the settings. Finally, the implement wouldn't turn on though he flipped the power switch a couple of times.

He returned the ancient detector to the tool shed and set it on the worktable. He'd rather repair this one, but he feared the device was beyond hope. It'd be worth getting a new one.

Austin headed for the door, and then he froze in place. Why hadn't he thought of this before? If Great Grandfather Jeremiah had buried treasure on the ranch, what if he didn't hide it in the pasture but somewhere in one of the ranch's buildings. The tool shed, the sheep barn, the horse barn. Maybe he'd even left some kind of reminder to himself as to where the treasure was. A map?

But then ... Austin wiped his brow and headed toward the ranch house for a frosty cold glass of lemonade. Maybe the whole gold thing was merely a rumor. Still, it wouldn't hurt to search the outbuildings.

Chapter Seventeen

Austin took a seat next to Mom and Mac in front of Dad's desk and inhaled a breath, waiting for his father to speak.

"It's that time again. Time for our annual boys' home barbeque fundraiser." Dad lifted his chin, a proud smile on his face. "This will be our fifteenth annual barbeque. Diane and Betsy will be in charge of the food, but I'll need Mac and you, Austin, to help set up, monitor the games and petting zoo, and serve wherever necessary."

Mom beamed. "I always love preparing the barbecue. I'm grateful Betsy is available to help since Jace and Charlotte will be out of town."

Austin hiked his leg over his knee. "Will Peyton and Erica be here this year?"

Dad nodded. "Definitely, and Peyton's father as well."

Mom's face sobered. "What would you think of

diverting some of the funds to the Horse Haven Boys' Ranch?"

Dad scribbled something on his notepad. "I like the idea, but I want to avoid anything that looks like nepotism. If any of us want to contribute to the boys' ranch, we can do it privately."

"You're right." Mom smiled.

"But I promised Willow Lawson, thirty percent of the proceeds to rebuild her practice, and of course the remaining funds to the boys' home in Oakville."

Later after Dad concluded the meeting, Austin walked toward the horse barn to check on Jack. He pulled out his cell phone and called Willow's number. The perfect time to remind her about the good news.

~

Austin smiled down at the lovely woman by his side as they exited the restaurant's patio.

Willow glanced behind her. "The outdoor seating area under the oaks was so romantic, and the Old Mill's brisket and potato salad was better than I've had in ages."

He squeezed her hand. "It was delicious, but wait till you taste Mom's barbecue at the fundraiser."

Her eyes twinkled with excitement. "Speaking of the fundraiser, your family's gift was incredibly meaningful to me. I'm honored. I can't thank all of you enough."

Austin chuckled. "This is the first year Dad's designated some of the funds to another cause besides the boys' home." He tapped her shoulder and laughed. "You should feel privileged."

She reached for his hand on her shoulder. "I feel special. And, of course, I'll be there to help out the day of the fundraiser."

Austin restrained the urge to kiss her pink lips. He took a deep, calming breath, held the truck's passenger door for Willow, and got into the driver's seat.

Two doors down at the entrance to the local bar, someone caught Austin's attention. He stared out the window of his truck and then paused.

A scruffy-looking cowboy with a long-handled mustache and a Stetson pulled down over light brown hair jerked the bar door open and disappeared inside.

Austin stepped out of the truck. "Willow, lock the doors after I leave. I'll explain when I get back. Shouldn't take long."

She frowned. "All right."

What the guy was still doing in Oakville, Austin didn't know. If he were to guess, the straggler was up to no good.

Austin picked up his pace and approached the entrance to The Watering Hole. He walked into the darkened room, smoke hanging in the air. He maneuvered his way past the bar to the tables toward the back of the room, scrutinizing every person. No sign of the dubious cowboy. Could he have spotted someone else who looked like the guy at the ranch?

Two women sat at a table next to the wall, one puffing on a cigarette.

"Hey, cowboy." The second winked at him. "Wanta join us."

Austin stiffened his shoulders. Giving the impression he was there to pick up a date was the last thing he wanted to do. "No, thanks."

On the back wall, a door which likely led to the out-of-doors remained closed. But spending more time in the smoke-infested room didn't appeal to him.

Turning around to head toward the entrance, he walked into the cool night, breathing in the fresh air. Why had he decided to search for the guy anyway? Stupid idea.

He opened his truck door and glanced at Willow. "I'm sorry to have left you, but I saw someone I wanted to check out. A guy who came to apply for a job at the ranch the other day. I saw him walking into that bar. I would've thought he'd left town by now."

"I take it you didn't hire him."

"No. I investigated the facts he'd given us. All false. Dad and I both had a bad feeling about him."

Willow gripped his arm as he sat down into the passenger's seat. "Do you suppose he had anything to do with the digging on your property?"

He stared at her for a moment. "I don't know why I didn't think of that."

Chapter Eighteen

Austin glanced at the trees growing over the driveway and clenched his teeth. The leafy limbs caught on their vehicles every time and needed to be trimmed soon. Since the chainsaw had finally given up, it was time to replace it. He headed to Logan's Home Improvement in town.

He parked in front of the store, turned off the ignition, and rested his head on the steering wheel. Willow's words had raced through his thoughts all week and then into the weekend. Could the grungy cowboy who'd applied for a job at the ranch have been the culprit who dug holes in the pasture—or the person who ransacked Willow's clinic? And what would've been the motive?

Since Austin hadn't seen the dubious character since that night at the bar, maybe he'd moved on. But if he had committed a crime here in Oakville, would he not have to pay for what he did?

Austin headed toward the entrance of the large box store. Through his short-sleeved shirt, the warmth from the June sun soaked into his skin. He couldn't ask for a more beautiful day. Central Texas was perfect this time of year. The blue and violet lupine growing along the road into town seem to lift the pressure of the difficulties his family faced.

Austin navigated the aisles until he arrived at the tool section. Rows of chainsaws were displayed on sturdy shelves. One orange and black model caught the glow of the bright overhead lights.

"Can I help you, sir." The clerk with a sturdy green apron and jeans arrived at his side.

"I need the best chainsaw you have for cutting tree branches." Austin picked up the saw and turned it over in his hand.

"You're holding a mid-range model which should work well for your purposes."

"Great. I'll take it." Austin put the tool in his cart and glanced around.

"Can I help you with anything else?"

"Yes, I need a metal detector."

The clerk checked his handheld computer. "Hmm. Just what I thought. We're out, and the store's next shipment hasn't arrived yet. Seems they're a popular item these days. Two guys came in looking for metal detectors several weeks ago."

No metal detectors. Two men purchasing both of them? Strange.

"I can call you when they come in. Leave your name and number at the information desk."

"Thanks, I will." Austin glanced at his cart and headed to the front of the store. Then he made a U-turn, approaching the clerk again. "Do you remember the two?"

The clerk scratched his head. "Yes, I waited on them. I remember them because as I recall, I'd never seen those two around here before. Two middle aged guys. If I were to guess I'd say they worked as ranch hands."

~

Willow gathered her cleaning bucket and set it inside Emma's front entrance.

Emma drew her into a hug. "My sweet girl. How can I ever thank you? Coming over here, cleaning my house, and bringing me groceries."

Willow returned her hug. "You aren't able to do it yourself, so I'm more than happy to. My schedule at the pet store doesn't keep me as busy as the clinic did."

Emma dropped into a chair in her living room. She set her basket with her knitting supplies on the side table. "Speaking of that, has the sheriff made any headway on finding out who destroyed your equipment?"

"I'm afraid not. They give me an update once a week. Last week, they said they were gathering information that could lead to solving the case."

"In the meantime, you sit and wonder."

Willow relaxed into the chair near Emma's. "I've had some progress with the insurance company, though. After they sent the inspector, they said I'd likely hear something in a month."

Emma reached out and rubbed her hand. "Sweetie, I'm so sorry you had to come to Texas and run into this kind of trouble."

"Thank you. Sometimes, I wonder if I did the right thing moving here, but then I had my reasons as you know."

Emma brushed a strand of her long, gray hair from her cheek. An expression filled her face, one that Willow couldn't read. "May I ask? Are you and Austin …?"

"I know what you're asking. No one could take the place of your son in my life. Ever." She squeezed Emma's hand. "I want you to be sure of that. But, yes, Austin and I have become closer recently. Though I miss Jesse with all my heart, I believe I could be falling for Austin Ford."

"I've only seen him from a distance and that was at the feed store in town. I asked the clerk if he knew him, and he said yes, he was one of the Ford clan. His, er, similarity to Jesse startled me. It's uncanny."

Willow searched Emma's face. What else was she saying? "The first time I saw him, I, well, I have to admit, I fainted."

Emma clapped her hand over her mouth. "If it weren't so serious, I'd laugh."

Willow swallowed and braved the question. "Emma, is there anything you haven't told me?"

Emma bit her lip and slowly nodded. "Yes." Her gaze lingered straight ahead over Willow's shoulder. "I want to, but the situation is very complicated. I'm baffled and have no facts. Can you forgive me?"

Willow frowned, shaking her head. "Of course." But what was Emma not saying? Did she actually have two children? Yet, she'd said Jesse was her only child. Could Austin actually be her son, Jesse's brother? But then, why wasn't Emma willing to tell her?

Willow rose and reached over to kiss Emma's cheek. No matter what happened, she loved her.

After an hour, Willow turned to leave, grasping her bucket.

Emma blew her a kiss. "I love you, my dear child. Thank you so much."

Chapter Nineteen

Willow giggled as the little lamb rubbed its soft muzzle against her palm, its fluffy white wool glowing in the late afternoon sun. She caught a whiff of the smoky sweet ribs braising on the grill. Austin sidled up to her side and placed a playful kiss on her cheek, making her pulse pound.

"My parents have raised money for the boys' home for as long as I can remember. The crowds, the tasty food, the petting zoo ..." Austin slipped his hand around her waist. "But this is the first time a beautiful woman like you has attended."

Willow's pulse raced in her veins, Austin's words resonating in her heart. She smiled and looked over at the animal cage. "This might be my favorite part," she said. "All those lambs. They must be close to being weaned by now."

"Yes, they're from the flock born this year." He turned his head toward the crowd filling the area in front of the main house. "Did you see Mac reading to the younger children who came from the home? I get a kick out of the burly guy sitting on a low stool with the little kids gathered around him."

"Yes, and I saw your mom painting little faces at a booth closer to the house. Austin, I love it."

Heading around the corner of the house, an attractive blond-haired woman in jeans, cowboy hat, and pony tail approached, followed by a good-looking man. As they neared, Willow recognized them. Erica and Peyton.

Erica held out her hand. "Good to see you again, Willow."

Peyton shook her hand. "How are things going with getting your clinic up and running?"

"Every day, I'm getting closer to opening. I still can't thank you all enough for helping me. I never dreamed something like a break-in would happen to me, but it did. Having you all there meant everything." Maybe someday she'd have a chance to help them out.

Erica leaned closer to Willow. "Has the sheriff made any progress on finding the culprit?"

Willow shook her head. "Not yet." Heat filled her cheeks. Would the criminals ever be brought to justice? Sometimes, anger and doubt threatened to control her. She allowed the summer breeze to calm her nerves.

"Give it time. The perpetrators will go to jail soon enough," Erica patted her arm. "I guarantee it."

Willow peered at the grass under her feet for a moment. She wished she could feel as confident as Austin's sister.

Erica tugged Willow's arms. "I could use a break from all the hustle around here, and we have such a beautiful day today. You want to walk over to Austin's helicopter pad and scout out the area? Besides, I'd like to get to know you a little better."

Erica's warm smile radiated assurance, replacing Willow's apprehension and making her feel like a part of the family. She waved to Peyton and Austin and then gently guided Willow toward the hard-packed road that ran past the main house, the same path Austin had taken when they visited the north pasture.

"I'm proud of my brother for getting his helicopter license. Took a while to convince Dad that he could round up sheep just as efficiently as on horseback."

Willow didn't want to mention the night Austin used his helicopter to locate unwanted visitors in the north pasture.

Erica chuckled. "And then there are the times when Fred, the donkey, isn't on duty—Austin swoops over the herd to chase away predators."

Ahead, a flat, circular surface constructed of reinforced concrete with a large H in the middle became visible.

Erica cleared her throat. "We've talked enough about me. How about you? You're from California?"

"Yes, but I moved to Oakville when my husband died." Willow twirled a strand of her hair around her finger before letting it fall free. "My mother-in-law lives here. Do you know Emma Lawson?"

Erica scratched her head. "Hmm. I don't believe I do."

"She doesn't leave the house very often due to her arthritis. I help her out as much as I can."

Erica turned to Willow and grasped her hands. "I'm so very pleased my brother is dating you. He couldn't have picked a nicer lady."

Willow's cheeks turned pink. "I've got my fair share of flaws, that's for sure. But thanks. I can't even imagine what it's like for you and your siblings to have such a deep connection to the place, all coming from the original owner, Jeremiah Ford."

Clang, clang.

"We better get back to the house. That's the signal that the meal is about to be served."

Willow matched Erica's brisk stride as they headed to the ranch. She couldn't imagine a better friend than Austin's sister. But she wasn't able to shake the thought—when Erica learned about Jesse's resemblance to her brother and the circumstances of his birth, would she still be so accepting?

~

Austin rose from the long picnic table, nodded

at the rancher seated across from him, and looked around for Willow. Since she'd volunteered to help with the cleanup, she was probably in or near the kitchen.

Dad tightly clutched the black, leather bag he used to hold the proceeds and walked toward Austin. He winked. "Your mom and I really like this new lady in your life." He slapped Austin on the back. "You made a good choice there, son. She'll be pleased to know her thirty percent share of the proceeds is fairly substantial. The funds will go a long way in supporting her as she works to reopen her clinic. Oakville Boys' Home will receive a hefty sum this year as well."

Austin's insides did a summersault. "Thanks, Dad. I know she appreciates it. And I'm grateful for the way our family has welcomed her."

The sun slowly slid under the horizon. "Always amazes me how stars seem to shine brighter out here in the country." Austin searched the crowd one more time for a sign of Willow.

Dad pointed toward the kitchen door. "Looking for our new vet? I see her over there with a pile of serving dishes in her hands."

Austin exhaled a deep sigh and walked toward her. "Thanks for helping. I'm going to do a routine security check in the ATV. I wanted to make sure you'll still be here when I get back."

A soft smile played on Willow's lips, as if she enjoyed the simple pleasure of a family gathering. "Let me deliver these dishes to the kitchen, and I'll go with you. Your mom and Erica are almost finished with the cleanup."

"Sure." Austin's heart picked up speed. The connection they shared was undeniable, even inseparable, he hoped. He tucked the sense of comfort in her presence away in his heart to ponder another time.

Willow returned from the kitchen, gripped his hand, and laughed. "If we run into any danger out there, I'm sure you'll protect me. Either you or that donkey that guards the sheep."

"You mean Fred?" Austin chuckled. "Coyotes or wolves are out of luck. Fred scares them off every time." He led Willow through the backyard and toward the road where he'd left the ATV.

Although the day had been warm, a soft breeze brushed against his neck, offering refreshing relief with the fading light. He helped Willow into the vehicle and took the road to the north pasture. While he didn't want to worry Willow, a nagging thought pestered him for the past hour. Could the intruders have learned about the event and chosen this moment to return? He shook his head, dismissing the idea. No, he was being paranoid.

Willow sighed. "I can't thank you and your family enough for inviting me and sharing the proceeds."

"Dad said the profits were better than usual.

Your portion will be a great help when you're ready to begin purchasing equipment again."

"Which should be soon." She laughed. "I got a notice from the insurance company that my reimbursement should arrive in the next couple of weeks. Of course, the funds won't completely cover everything, so the Fords' contribution will make up the difference."

Austin brought the vehicle to a halt in the vicinity where they'd last spotted signs of digging.

To the left, the grove of trees at the edge of the Ford property loomed like a natural sanctuary. The rustling leaves whispered softly in the night breeze, infusing the area with a sense of tranquility.

Willow followed him to the trees. "Has the sheriff been around?"

"Yes, at least twice a week. Seems that every time he pays us a visit, the intruders seem to disappear."

Willow grasped his hand again. "Like they have a sixth sense about the area."

"Or they sniff out the sheriff and run off." Austin clicked on his flashlight and directed the beam toward a mound of dirt he didn't remember seeing before. He walked closer, releasing Willow's hand. A hole about four feet lay adjacent to the mound. He shined the light into the hole. "Look at this, Willow. There're some coins in the bottom of this hole." He bent down to retrieve them. "Two nickels, a dime and a quarter."

Nothing from Willow.

He turned around and swallowed hard, tension rising in his throat.

In the shadow of the tree, a figure shrouded in darkness, with a ball cap pulled low over his face, pressed a rough hand over Willow's mouth.

"Mm." She squirmed but remained in the perpetrator's clutches.

"Hey." Anger surged within Austin. "Let her go." He growled. Of all the times not to bring his handgun.

"Give me the map, or she gets hurt." A man's muffled voice spoke from under what Austin now recognized as a mask.

"What are you talking about? If you don't release her—"

The person took a few steps backward into the trees, dragging Willow's petite frame with him.

Fury exploded in Austin's chest. He dove for the man's feet, knocking him to the ground as Willow escaped the man's hold. The stench of stale tobacco and alcohol gagged him.

Willow yelped and raced toward the ATV.

The man scrambled up and darted into the trees.

Austin gritted his teeth. Either chase after the man or make sure Willow was okay.

He caught up with her and pulled her into his arms. "I'm so sorry." He closed his eyes, feeling her warmth next to him. He never wanted harm to come to her. He had to protect her, even if it meant putting himself in danger.

Willow trembled, clearly gripped by fear. "I'm okay." She rested her head on his chest.

Austin clenched his teeth hard. "It should never have happened to you in the first place, especially on Ford property." He pulled out his cell phone and punched in 9-1-1. "The intruder will likely be out of the area by the time the sheriff gets here, but at least we can report the incident."

Willow shook her head. "I can't believe I didn't remember my training."

"Your training?"

"Yes. I actually took a class in self-defense for women. But for some reason the perp caught me off guard."

With all his heart, he regretted that Willow had faced the attacker. But if the sheriff couldn't uncover who was intruding on their land, perhaps it was time for him to take matters into his own hands.

~

Willow stood on the front porch as Austin's parents went inside, leaving her and Austin to wrap things up with the sheriff.

The sheriff closed his notebook and tucked his pen into his pocket. "The perpetrator, when found, will be booked for assault as well as criminal trespassing.

Right now, we don't have a motive. Regardless, our department is doing everything we can to discover what's going on here."

Austin frowned. "He threatened me, saying I had to give him the map. Sheriff, the only thing I can guess is that he believes there's a treasure map around here somewhere."

The sheriff nodded. "We all know about the rumors of treasure on the Ford ranch. This guy might be one of the get-rich-quick characters who believe they'll find gold on your property. Or perhaps he's connected to the other perps who're digging back here. Or perhaps he's mentally unstable." The sheriff opened his notebook again and scribbled another note. "Still, why would he come to your ranch and attack an innocent woman?" Sheriff Banks patted Willow's arm and smiled at Austin. "Don't worry. We'll discover the truth about what's going on."

Like a bee sting to her arm, another concern nagged her. "Do you think that the incident tonight could be related to the destruction of my veterinarian clinic?"

The sheriff nodded. "My detectives and I will discuss the possibility. Let's continue to look for clues to any connections between you, Dr. Lawson, and the Ford Ranch. I'll be in touch." He turned toward his patrol car and got in.

Austin slid his arm around her waist. "Let's sit in the backyard on the swing for a while. I think we need some time to process this."

The reassuring pressure of Austin's arm around her offered protection. "As long as I'm with you, I feel safe." She gave him a half grin.

"In that case, I'm never letting you go." He kissed her cheek.

"I'm not sure what would've happened if you hadn't been there to overpower that jerk." Though this wasn't a laughing matter, she smiled and ran her hand along his strong biceps. "You've got some pretty nice muscles there."

A shy smile crept across Austin's face. "I'd do anything to protect you."

She followed him around the side of the house and to the backyard swing under the umbrella-shaped elm. On the horizon, the moon shone through a sliver of silvery cloud.

In the swing, Willow pushed her foot along the ground, sending the swing into motion. "Looking back now, I was terrified for a moment this evening, but in the midst of it all, God covered me with His peace. I felt a deep sense of confidence in the Lord's presence."

"The peace of God passes all understanding ..."

Willow smiled, appreciating Austin's reference to scripture. "The sheriff said he wanted to investigate the relationship between me and the Ford family. Do you think there's anything to that?"

"I'm not sure." Austin rubbed his chin. "I continue to ask myself—could my adoption into the family relate to you in anyway?"

If Willow were to guess, Austin referred to the way he looked so much like Jesse. But what would that have to do with her clinic? Confusion swirled in her mind like a thick fog. "I don't know, but one thing I'm sure of. Your parents love you very much. I believe children who've been adopted are greatly blessed because they are chosen by two people who truly care about their child."

Austin turned to look at her, a glimmer of moisture in his eyes. "Something I need to appreciate every day of my life."

A thought surfaced, one that began to slowly infiltrate her mind, sending a shiver to her body. She whispered, and her voice shook. "I don't know why I didn't think about this sooner." She took a deep breath. "When is your birthday?"

He stared at her a moment, and then repeated the month, day, and year.

Willow stopped breathing. Chills ran down her legs, and she froze, trying to assess the truth.

"Willow, are you okay?" He turned to her, clasping her shoulder.

She gripped his hand as hard as she could. "You won't believe this."

He raised his voice. "Willow, please tell me."

She could barely whisper, struggling to breathe. "That's Jesse's birthday—same month, day, and year."

Chapter Twenty

Before church, Austin placed the last breakfast plate in the dishwasher and pressed the start button.

Mom patted his shoulder. "You're the best son any mom could ask for. Thank you for helping this morning, sweetie."

Austin rose to a standing position. "There's something I need to ask you."

Mom hung her apron on the towel rack and slipped into the kitchen chair. With a look of concern, she gazed at him. "What is it?"

Austin sat beside her and cleared his throat. "When you adopted me, did Mr. Packard say there was another child?"

Mom laughed. "No. Adding one little baby boy to our family was about all your father and I could handle." Then her smile faded. "I'm sorry, honey. I can sense this is serious. Why do you ask?"

"Willow's dead husband, who looked exactly like me, I found out last night, we have the same birthdate, including the year."

"Oh, my." Mom gasped and her eyes went wide as she stared at him, her mouth slightly agape in surprise. "I can't understand it. As I mentioned before neither Mr. Packard nor the social worker ever told us about another child."

Austin lowered his voice to a whisper. "What else can I think. Jesse was not only my brother but my identical twin."

"You visited with Mr. Packard, correct?" Mom asked.

"Yes, and he wasn't able to reveal anything except he'd met my birthmother, and at the time she was in good health."

Mom covered his hand with hers. "We all need to put this in God's hands. If there are answers we don't have now, God can provide them if He believes it necessary."

Austin's heart warmed at his mother's pure faith in God. He should take a lesson from her. "Mr. Packard said something unusual. He said he figured I'd find the answers I seek someday, but they wouldn't come from him."

Mom's gentle kiss on his cheek eased the turmoil swirling in his stomach.

~

Willow stepped out of the cowboy church and into the splendor of the summer day. Her heart quickened as Austin grasped her hand, warmth spreading from his touch.

"You ready for lunch?" Austin's green eyes held her gaze, drawing her in with their quiet intensity.

She patted her stomach. "I'm starved."

At the truck's passenger door, Austin's hand tightened gently on her arm, his touch halting her in place. "I told my mother about Jesse's birthday. Again, she assured me she knew nothing about a sibling."

"Since last night, I've thought of little else—the possibility of Jesse being your brother. There's something I haven't told you." She'd considered mentioning Emma to Austin before, but now it seemed imperative to tell him.

Austin helped her into the truck and marched around to the other side and got in. He paused, searching her face. "I'm listening."

"Do you remember I told you about Jesse's mother? She's a lovely woman named Emma."

He crinkled his brow. "I think so."

"One reason I moved to Oakville was to be where Jesse was born. A second reason was because his mother moved here as well."

His mouth fell open. "She lives here?"

"Yes."

Austin's jaw dropped. "I, er," He mumbled

something as he shook his head. Then he opened his mouth again. "If Jesse is my brother, then Emma has to be my birth mother."

"We don't know for sure that she had another child. She claims she didn't."

Austin slowly nodded and mumbled something again she couldn't discern.

Chills traveled up her spine as the possibility of the truth dawned on her. "Would you want to go with me to visit her?"

~

Austin's palms broke out with sweat as he followed Willow up the sidewalk to the modest home in an older section of Oakville. With each step, the implications tapped harder on his shoulder, until the possibilities spoke so loudly, he could no longer ignore them. "I'm not sure if this was a good idea."

Willow turned to face him. "I understand if you'd rather make this another time. Maybe I should've waited a few days to ask her if we could visit."

"After church—I should be fortified. I need to do this, but the situation is so bizarre. If I had a twin, why doesn't Mom know? She keeps insisting she has no idea about another child. And, like you said, Emma claims the same."

The front door eased open, and Austin's gaze lifted to the woman with long gray hair, leaning on two metal crutches. Her green eyes, so much like his own, peered at him. Then, as if snapping out of a dream, she shook her head. "Please, come in."

Willow by his side, he walked through the door to the humble living room furnished with old looking furniture.

Willow shot a nervous glance at Emma. "This is Austin Ford. Austin, Emma Lawson, my mother-in-law."

Emma gripped her crutches tightly, her breathing shallow. She hobbled into the living room and pointed to the couch. "Please sit down. May I get you something to drink?"

Willow sank into the worn fabric couch. "No, Emma. Thank you. We only wanted to chat a while."

Emma edged onto a straight-backed chair, not taking her eyes off Austin. "In the last few months that I've lived here, I've seen you in town at the store a couple of times. I didn't want to introduce myself as I felt awkward, but it's uncanny how much you look like my son Jesse."

"Thank you for seeing us today." Austin allowed his focus to remain on her a moment or two, not sure what else to say. The thought that she could be his biological mother sent waves of confusion crashing over him, each one raising unanswered questions. Yet he needed to get to the point. "Would you be comfortable if I ask some rather personal questions?"

"I've asked myself some of the same question

you're likely to ask me. I'll be happy to help in anyway."

Willow smiled. "This isn't easy on either of you. Thank you, Emma, for letting us visit you today."

Emma smiled at Willow in a way that assured Austin they were already friends, and that she felt completely at ease in her presence.

He searched for the confidence he needed to speak. "This may sound like a strange question, but when you gave birth to your son Jesse, did you have another child?" He released a quick breath. He'd laid everything on the line, praying for an answer that would finally bring the clarity he needed.

Emma folded her hands, nervously twisting an old-fashioned handkerchief between her fingers. "I want to be honest with you both." She glanced at Willow and back to him. "After Jesse was born, I thought it was all over. Then the doctor told me there was another baby. I gave birth to a second baby boy."

Willow lifted her hands in front of her and raised her voice. "But Emma, you told me you had a single birth."

"Please, let me finish." She dabbed her eyes with her handkerchief. "After my second child was born, the doctor took him away. He said my baby would never live longer than a week or so because he suffered from twin-to-twin transfusion syndrome. He received unequal levels of amniotic fluid and would pass away shortly." She covered her eyes, her shoulders shaking.

"So, wha...what happened?" Willow's voice was soft, fragile, like the whisper of the summer breeze.

Emma's sobs stole her words for a moment and then she gulped. "I signed over power of attorney for my second baby to Mr. Packard. He said when the time came, he'd handle the funeral and burial." With her weight shifted forward, she placed the crutches under her arms and slowly stood, balancing herself as she shuffled to Austin.

Austin stood up from his chair and opened his arms wide, catching Emma as she fell into him, enveloping her in an embrace.

"They told me you wouldn't live." She continued to cry. "I was afraid of the man who fathered Jesse—and you. I had to flee." She stood back and gazed into his eyes. "Austin, if I had known you would live, I never would've left you. You are a miracle of the Lord."

Austin fought to hold back the tears from falling down his cheeks, but his efforts were in vain. The warmth of Willow's body against his back enveloped him, her hands gently wrapping around Emma in a comforting embrace.

Finally, Emma sank back into her chair. "Every time I saw you in Oakville, I wondered ... But how could it be?" She pushed a long strand of hair from her face. "My second baby had died. You were someone who looked like Jesse." Her shoulders trembled once more, quaking with the weight of her emotions.

Austin's heart raced with a mix of anxiety and the quest for the truth. "To eliminate any doubt, we could consider taking a DNA test. It's just a thought, but what do you think?"

Chapter Twenty-One

Willow smiled as she took the lady's credit card and rang up the sale. "I think you'll be happy with the puppy food you purchased. And make sure you take her for regular walks."

The fluffy eight-week-old Goldendoodle gnawed on a chewy stick inside the pet carrier.

The customer picked up the carrier and laughed. "I think I'll name her Penny to match the color of her coat."

"I like that." Willow had to admit she was jealous. As soon as her clinic was up and running again, she wanted one of those friendly doodles. They would make a perfect addition to her veterinarian's office. "Mr. Roi allowed me to vaccinate her with her first shots, but she'll need her second round in about four more weeks."

"Thank you, Dr. Lawson. And I can't wait for you to open your clinic again."

Willow gazed toward the glass aquarium of goldfish and back to the customer. "I can't either. If I were to guess, I'd say I could be open by the time Penny needs her second set of shots. I finally settled with the insurance company, and thanks to a generous donation, I ordered my equipment. After everything arrives, there'll be the matter of setting up shop."

"Will you be in the same building?"

"Yes. The landlord has been very accommodating."

The new puppy mom, pet carrier in hand, headed toward the store's entrance.

As she approached, a man in uniform held the door for her to walk out.

Willow stared at the man. The sheriff?

He walked toward her. "Dr. Lawson, do you have a moment?"

She motioned to Mr. Roi. "Could you please man the desk for a few minutes?"

"Sure, Willow," her boss nodded and approached the counter.

Willow led the sheriff into the break room and turned to face him.

"Yes, sir?" Question after question shot through Willow's head as she faced Sheriff Banks. Did he have information? Would the perps be prosecuted?

The sheriff pulled a notebook out of his pocket, flipped a few pages, and glanced at the writing. "A day after the crime, my deputy retrieved several fingerprints from the crime scene. We recently got the results."

Willow's heart pounded. Finally, they'd have some answers and the trespassers would be brought to justice. She twisted her hands into tight balls.

The sheriff shook his head. "I'm afraid it wasn't good news. We checked several fingerprint databases and found two identifications. One was you and one was Chet Harris, your veterinarian tech. Two others, we didn't find matches for in the Texas system so we checked the national list maintained by the FBI. I'm sorry to say we didn't find any matches."

"Chet Harris would never willfully destroy my clinic so I suppose we're right back to where we started." Willow's hopes plummeted into her stomach.

"I'm afraid so, Dr. Lawson, as far as fingerprints go, but we're not giving up our investigation—and don't you either."

A weight pressed on her shoulders. "I'm trying to remain positive."

"I simply can't figure out why someone would ransack your clinic and warn you to leave the area. You've been nothing but a positive influence in our community. We need you here in Oakville."

~

Austin threw his heavy leather gloves on the workbench in the sheep pen and headed to the main house for lunch. The notice on the kitchen bulletin board after breakfast had perked up his interest. Tomato soup and grilled cheese sandwiches for today.

Mom eased into her chair in the kitchen and pointed to Austin's place across from Dad. A steaming bowl of soup and a sandwich with cheddar cheese oozing out the sides waited for him. "Only the three of us today. Mac took a sack lunch to the pasture to check on some of the flock grazing out there."

Austin bowed his head while Dad said a blessing. After the amen, Austin took a large bite of his sandwich. "As soon as I wrap up my inspection of the rest of the sheep, I'm heading to the pasture. I may need to get Willow out here to look at a couple of the ewes in the pen."

"What's going on?" Dad dipped his spoon into his soup.

"A couple of the younger ones appear to have difficulty walking—as if their limbs feel stiff, and they're having problems feeding." Austin sipped his iced tea.

Dad nodded. "I hope that girl gets her clinic open soon. We need her in town as well as on the ranches."

Mom dabbed her mouth with a napkin. "At least she can still make house and ranch calls."

Dad took another sip of soup. "You're right about that."

Austin swallowed hard. Was now a good time for him to approach his parents? "Dad, Mom, there're a few things I need to talk to you about." He set down his spoon next to the soup bowl.

Mom looked up from tomato soup to him. "You know you can talk to us about anything."

Though Dad remained silent, he trained his gaze on Austin's face.

Austin cleared his throat. "After church yesterday, Willow and I paid a visit to her mother-in-law, Emma Lawson."

"I remember a Lawson family, but I believe they both passed away after a car wreck." Dad said.

Austin nodded. "Yes, that was Emma's parents. Emma had moved away to California as a young adult but returned a few years ago."

"You said she is Willow's mother-in-law?" Mom placed her napkin in her lap.

"Yes, and get ready. This is a life changer." Since he was still continuing to process the notion that Emma was his biological parent, Mom and Dad would likely have trouble as well.

Mom's gaze caught Austin's and didn't release him. He had to reveal the truth to his parents. He took a deep breath and gripped his hands into a tight fist. "She's my biological mother."

Mom and Dad stared at Austin as if he'd told them he'd just returned from a trip to the moon. For the next thirty minutes, he relayed the story to his parents. "Emma didn't believe her second baby had survived, and Mr. Packard never told you about her first. It's been a mystery until recently. I'm grateful the truth has come to the surface, but in my heart, you are both my parents."

Mom dabbed at a tear in her eye. "This is a lot to take in. I suppose Mr. Packard was right. You found out the facts, yet not through him." She placed her hand on his. "You've gone through so much lately. I pray things will settle down soon. But nothing has really changed. You are now and always will be our son."

Dad snickered. "Well, you said you had a couple of things to talk about. I can't imagine the next item of business will be as monumental as this."

Austin smiled, grateful that Dad had lightened the serious moment. "Yes. It's about the intruders. No doubt, they're looking for something on the ranch. The only logical answer is they've heard the rumors of buried treasure that have spread through the years—that it's somewhere on our property."

Dad shook his head. "Makes sense. But recently, our family hasn't made any effort to search for it. While your grandfather was running the ranch, he was preoccupied with my sister's passing and other family matters."

Mom grasped Dad's arm as if to stop him. "Remember before Tim went off to medical school, he'd thought about the story. He spent some time searching the north pasture and even did some digging closer to the house. He had plans to look in the west pasture after that. He never found anything."

Austin took a bite of the sandwich and glanced at both Mom and Dad. "Would you object if I continued to search?"

"Of course, not." Dad smiled. "But I'm afraid you're wasting your time."

"You're probably right, but what if you were to explore the ranch, what would be your first step?"

Dad smiled. "I'd check for a map. There were reports that Grandpa Jeremiah had become somewhat forgetful. I would expect he'd leave some sort of record in case he couldn't remember where he hid the gold. Or perhaps he wanted someone in our family to find it." Dad threw up his hands. "That is if there really was a treasure hoard."

Austin leaned closer to Dad. "Any guesses as to where I should start?"

"Tell you what, son. The storage closet in my office has a lot of old ranch records. You might want to start there."

Austin tapped his forehead and groaned. "Could be a huge job. Do you mind if I ask Willow to help me?"

~

Willow knocked on the ranch office door and then stepped in.

A pile of boxes was stacked near a storage closet on the opposite wall from Mr. Ford's desk. "You started without me." She chuckled.

Austin glanced up. "I promise dinner tonight as a thank you. Betsy's cooking, and I believe she's making cordon bleu."

"All right. It's a deal." Willow glanced around the office. "What do you have so far?"

He pointed to the stacked boxes. "Those are all dated. One for every year the ranch has been in operation."

An idea began to form in her mind. "Your great-grandfather Jeremiah established the ranch before the depression, is that true?"

"That's correct. Before that time, Jeremiah had accumulated wealth by investing in gold."

"Hmm. That's beginning to make sense." As she'd suspected, he was coping with the challenges of the depression. "So, he hid his wealth on this ranch somewhere known only to him."

"True. But there're rumors about a map. If we could find one ..." Austin's grin filled his face.

Willow scratched her head. "Speaking of maps, I've been thinking about our intruders and the way they've only dug in one spot. Do you suppose they have a map of some kind indicating treasure in the north pasture?"

"I've asked Dad about the possibility, and he can't figure out how they might've acquired a map." He folded his arms over his chest. "But in Great Grandfather Ford's case, there's a good chance he left one. Our task is to see if we can find it."

"Okay, let's go to work. Let me get this clear. We're looking for any clues or perhaps a map of where treasure could be hidden here at the ranch."

"That's it." Austin leaned toward her, rubbing his hands together, obviously ready to move forward. "If you'd like to go through the boxes with labels beginning in the mid-forties, I'll bring the rest of the boxes out. I'd like to see what else I can find in the dark recesses of that closet."

Willow dragged the first box down and placed it in the center of the room. She sat cross-legged on the floor and thumbed through the old documents. Pages listing an inventory of pull plows, seed drills, and a combine filled the records. She breathed in the dust from the century old documents and sneezed.

After fifteen minutes, she moved the box to the side and brought the next one in front of her. "Box one is done and no clues."

"All the boxes are out, and the closet is empty." He set the box nearest him on the floor and began thumbing through the papers.

After an hour, Willow stood to stretch her legs. Toward the back of the current box, something besides files of papers caught her eye. She reached in. "Look at this, Austin." She retrieved a book with a worn leather cover. The spine was frayed, and toward the top right, *Jeremiah Ford* was engraved in gold letters.

Austin widened his eyes, and he reached to take

the book in his hand. "I think you have something here." He eased onto the couch. "Sit next to me."

Willow took a seat next to Austin as he read aloud. Page after page of his great-grandfather's journal painted a picture of life in the forties. After fifteen minutes, Austin stopped and pointed to the entry on Wednesday, June 19, 1940.

Willow read, "Yesterday's newspaper said that those scoundrels are getting desperate. Bandits will stop at nothing. I fear for my possessions, especially my gold pieces which will see us through our later years. I've decided to bury them behind the ranch house under the river birch close to the smoke house." Her voice stumbled over the words. "Austin, that's it. The treasure is buried out back, not in the north pasture."

Austin shook his head. "The old ranch house is gone now, and I'm pretty sure the river birch doesn't grow there anymore."

"That's okay. We can still identify the general area. Do you have a metal detector?"

"Yes, finally. Logan's Home Improvement was out, but I found one at the small hardware store in town."

Austin needed a breakthrough about the buried treasure—something definitive, either a yes or a no. "We need God's direction."

"Amen." Austin rose from the couch. "I'm going out to the tool shed to get the detector and a couple of shovels. Do you mind doing a little digging?"

"Of course not." She raised her arm as she flexed her muscles. "If I can manage horses Jack's size, I can dig a few holes. I'll wait here and read a few more entries until you get back."

Willow leaned against the couch and sighed. Life in the 1940s fascinated her.

She continued turning the pages, journeying through the months. She read the entry on December 10, 1948 and gasped. "Decided not to risk keeping the gold in the backyard anymore. I moved it to another place and made a map in case my aging brain fails me. The map is—" Willow paused and turned the page. Nothing there.

Austin trudged through the outer office door. "I have the tools. You ready?"

Willow shook her head. "You need to read this." She held up the journal to him.

Austin glanced at the book and then looked up at her. "That's crazy. So where did he move it? And why didn't he finish the entry? If only we had those answers."

"Austin, the rest of the journal is blank. There's nothing after December 10 of 1948."

"Come with me." Austin led Willow outside to the horse barn. "I have an idea."

Inside Mr. Ford shoed a horse and then looked up. "Austin and Willow. What's going on? From the look on your faces, you ran into a problem."

"Dad, do you know when Great Grandpa

Jeremiah died."

Mr. Ford rubbed his chin. "Hmm. I believe it was in 1948. Right before Christmas. I remember Grandpa Martin telling us kids what a sad holiday they had that year." He scratched his head. "Yes, that was it. He died on December 11, 1948.

Chapter Twenty-Two

Austin picked the last of the green peppers from the garden next to the house and then waved as Willow's van approached from the main highway.

Mac exited the bunk house walking toward him. "I'm going to the kitchen to help your mom with dinner prep since Betsy's off, but I can work in the garden for a while if you'd like."

"Thanks, Mac. Mom said she was making stuffed bell peppers tonight. I'd appreciate it if you'd run these into the kitchen."

"Sure, thing." Mac took the basket from Austin and walked toward the house and then paused. "Hey, buddy. Is there something going on between you and the new vet? Okay, so I'm being noisy."

Austin waved him off. "Aww, we're just taking things slow right now." If his growing interest in Willow was becoming too obvious, perhaps he should pull back. He frowned. But everyone had noticed when

Erica and Peyton fell in love. Sure, Willow was new in town, but so was Peyton back then. Why should he keep from pursuing a relationship with her? He threw up his hands in confusion.

Willow parked her van in front of the house and got out.

Austin's pulse picked up a pace or two. Her long brown hair hung around her petite shoulders. Even the sway of her hips when she ambled closer got his attention. He shook his head and mumbled. "Get it together, Ford."

"Dinner was delicious last night. Thanks for inviting me again tonight." She held out a pan. "I brought brownies. I hope they fit in with what your mom's cooking."

"You bet. And thank you for coming over to help me search again. You found the journal. We should be able to find the map." He folded his arms over his chest. "Besides, we've got to locate the treasure before some intruder gets to it."

Willow rolled her eyes. "If we do find a map, I hope we'll be able to decipher the clues left by a rancher one hundred years ago."

~

Helping Austin discover the mystery of a hidden map sounded exciting, but at the same time challenging. Yet Willow had to admit, the search meant she could spend more time with him. Her growing feelings for Austin spurred her on.

Austin scratched his head. "You're right. Who knows what went on in Great Grandpa Jeremiah's head. He could've hidden the map anywhere."

"So, nothing remains of his home?"

Austin shook his head. "Jeremiah's house was demolished years ago when Dad built this house. Dad stored all the old ranch records in the boxes we searched yesterday."

"We didn't come across anything resembling a treasure map." Willow sighed. "Do you think Jeremiah kept other papers in another location?"

"Not to my knowledge, but I can check with Dad. Maybe a lockbox at the bank or something. But in the meantime, I think our best approach is to search the outer buildings on the ranch. The sheep barn, the horse barn, tool shed, everywhere."

Willow tapped her palm to her forehead. "Sounds like a big job, but there're only so many places on this ranch he could hide a map. Where do you want to start?"

"How about the machinery shop. We have a couple of hours before dinner." He glanced toward the prefab storage building and then paused. "Wait. Grandpa Marvin and Dad have replaced most of the outer buildings through the years." He fiddled with the top button on his shirt. "This could be a hopeless venture."

"They may have torn down the old buildings, but I'm sure they didn't discard the original farming implements and other tools—or anything else that appeared to be valuable."

"You're right. But in any case, our odds of finding a map could be pretty slim."

Willow placed a gentle hand on his arm. "I think we better turn this whole thing over to the Lord."

Warmth spread through Austin's insides. She'd reminded him of the most essential Source of help. After an hour's search through the up-to-date storage room amidst tractors, a couple of ATVs, an old truck, and a mower, Austin wiped the sweat off his forehead. "I have an idea. I haven't had a good visit with Grandpa Martin and Grandma Teresa in a while. Would you want to go with me tomorrow?"

Willow gave him a high five. "I'd like to meet them, and maybe Grandpa Martin will remember something your father didn't."

Chapter Twenty-Three

Grandpa and Grandma Ford's simple, quiet house always brought Austin a sense of peace and excitement. How many times as a child had he come for a fun day filled with making cookies with Grandma and sitting on Grandpa's lap, reading a book? He always loved looking through Grandma's scrapbooks, too.

Austin held the door for Willow as she stepped out of his truck. Compared to his childhood, he didn't visit as often as he'd like these days.

Willow gazed up at him, the vision of her creamy skin and sparkling eyes setting his heart pacing faster. "Every turn of this mission's a challenge, like fitting pieces of a puzzle together."

"I hope one day we finally find all the parts." Austin smiled and rang the doorbell. "They will like you as much as I—" He grinned and snapped his mouth shut. Not exactly the best time to tell her how much he cared about her.

The door opened, and Grandma stepped out onto the porch, her arms open wide. "Oh, my sweet Austin. It's been too long." She hugged Austin and then gazed at Willow. "And who is this pretty girl?"

Austin scolded himself as heat rose to his cheeks. What was he, twelve? To allow her comment to embarrass him was ridiculous. "Grandma, this is Willow Lawson. She's Oakville's new veterinarian."

Grandma pulled Willow into her arms. "Welcome to Oakville, dear. I'm sorry to hear about your clinic."

"Nice to meet you, Grandma Teresa. It will be up and running again soon. No more than a month, I'm hoping."

Grandma swept her hands toward the door. "Come in, you two, and say hi to Grandpa."

As usual, his grandfather sat in a recliner facing the TV. He turned and held his hand out to Austin. "Forgive me, son, if I don't get up. Feeling a little weak today."

Austin reached down to give his grandpa a hug. "And this is my friend, Willow."

Grandma pointed to the couch. "You two get comfortable, and I'll be back with cold drinks."

At Grandpa Martin's age, his health concerned Austin. "Have you been to a doctor about your condition?" He edged down beside Willow on the couch.

"You know those doctors. They send you home

with a bottle of pills and tell you to come back in a month. I'm doing fine. Grandma Teresa is feeding me healthy food, and I'll be back to my normal self before we know it."

Austin scratched his head. His grandfather was aging which Austin didn't want to admit sometimes. "Other than being a little tired, how have you been?"

Grandpa pointed to some photo albums on the cabinet to his right. "Been taking a couple of trips down memory lane. Me and your grandma were looking at the pictures of the ranch from way back before your time."

Austin's heart picked up speed. "Do you have any pictures from when Great Grandpa Jeremiah first bought the ranch?"

"I believe there are some. You and that pretty lady help yourselves. Look through any you'd like."

Austin rose from his seat, picked up a couple of scrapbooks, and set them between him and Willow. "Do you remember anything about Great Grandfather Jeremiah hiding a map which showed where he'd buried gold pieces?"

Grandpa folded his arms over his chest. "He was somewhat of a cheapskate. I wouldn't have put it past him."

Willow gave him an excited grin and glanced toward Grandpa again.

Grandpa went on, "But no, he never mentioned anything about gold. I did overhear him a couple of times talking to my mom about where to hide an important paper. He never said exactly what kind of paper, but I always assumed he might have been referring to a map of some kind. After my dad passed, though, I stopped giving it much thought."

Austin sat forward in his chair. "When you and Grandma ran the ranch, did you find any clues as to where a map might be hidden?"

"No, not really." Grandpa sat back in his recliner, folding his hands in his lap. "Some of the town folks spread rumors concerning gold pieces buried out on the ranch. But I didn't pay much attention. I had my hands full with running the ranch and raising the kids. After Rebecca died, we spent most of our time taking care of your father and the ranch chores. I'm sorry I can't be more of a help."

"Who would like some sweet tea and sugar cookies?" Grandma set two glasses of tea in front of them on the coffee table and a large plate of cookies. She passed Grandpa a glass and giggled. "He's watching his sugar so he doesn't get any cookies, only unsweetened tea."

"Awe, Teresa, I could eat just one."

"Nope." Grandma sat down in the easy chair adjacent to the couch. "You young people look through those albums if you'd like."

Willow took a bite of the cookie and opened the first album. After thumbing through a couple of pages, she pointed to a set of pictures. "These must be photos of the old equipment building before your father took it down. The prefab building stands there now."

Austin leaned closer and gazed over her shoulder. He pointed to the horse barn. "This one's new also. And so is bunk house."

Willow turned the page and stared at the next set of pictures. "Looks like the sheep barn might be the original building."

"And the tool shed as well as the corral around the sheep barn."

Austin took a long sip of tea and peered at the album. What clue did the book hold? When Dad built new buildings to replace the older ones, he would've remembered finding a document such as a handwritten map, yet his father had recalled nothing. Was it likely that the map would be hidden in one of Jeremiah's original buildings on the ranch?

~

The sun dipped low on the horizon as Willow walked alongside Austin, leaving his grandparents' house behind and heading toward the truck parked on the street. A warm summer breeze lifted her spirits.

The welcoming atmosphere of the home wrapped around Willow like a familiar hug. She sighed. She'd never known her grandparents. And her own parents had died all too soon.

"Before I take you home, how about a short trip

to our city park? It's a beautiful evening." Austin stuck his key into the ignition.

"I'd love it. Besides, we need some time to debrief. If we brainstorm a while, we might be able to piece together the facts and figure out a better way to search for the map—that is if there is a map."

The setting sun cast low beams of golden light across the old brick building on Main Street. Where the business district ended, tall oaks loomed over a sprawling patch of vegetation, while scattered pole lamps along the paved path flickered to life.

Austin stopped on one side of the street close to the park. Stepping from the driver's side of the truck, he helped her out, and they trekked down the walkway onto a path through the trees. The trail wound through live oaks, cedar elm, and Texas ash. Then the soothing flow of water caught her attention.

Austin placed his hand on her back and led her to an ornate metal bench. "You'll enjoy this."

Ahead, a small waterfall cascaded over a series of sandstone layers, the water gurgling as it splashed and tumbled into a stream below.

Willow clutched her throat. "This is a hidden oasis in the middle of the town."

Austin chuckled. "I figured you'd like it."

On the metal seat, Willow snuggled next to Austin. "You have a great family. Your parents and now I got to meet your grandparents."

"I've always felt blessed to have such an

awesome mom and dad. I'm not sure where my life would be right now if they hadn't adopted me."

Willow sighed. "God was looking out for you."

"He does the same for you, Willow." He smoothed his hand over hers.

Though she didn't want to admit it, Austin's touch brought comfort and warmth. Then the thought struck her like the intruder on Austin's ranch, gripping her with a firm hold. What if she only saw Austin as a substitute for Jesse?

She straightened and shifted away from him on the bench, creating space between them.

"What's wrong?" Austin's expression was etched with desperation.

"I care for you so much. Actually, I think I'm falling in love with you."

"You don't know how much that mean to me." Austin reached toward her. "But what's the look on your face—as if you were horrified?"

She covered her eyes with her hands, not daring to gaze at him. "What if my emotions and my mind are playing tricks on me? What if I'm merely looking for a substitute for Jesse?"

She let her hands fall away and studied his expression. She'd never seen him look so sad.

Austin opened his mouth and then closed it again, slowly shaking his head. He whispered. "I need to tell you the truth. I'm falling in love with you, too. But I could never replace my brother in your life and don't want to." He sighed, turning away from her. When he faced her again, moisture had settled in the corners of his eyes. "What are you saying? You don't want to be with me anymore?"

Willow delved deep into her soul. "All my adult life, I've known that love is never a straightforward matter. There are always risks." She shook her head hard and brushed a tear out of her eye. "But, Austin, the thought of never seeing you again—it tears my heart apart. I'm willing to take the risk."

Austin pulled her into his arms and held her. "So am I."

For several moments she basked in his embrace. Then she opened her eyes.

A figure with dark curly hair poking out from beneath a grimy ball cap darted from behind a tree and raced down the sidewalk.

Chapter Twenty-Four

Austin worked the curry comb through Jack's hair from his neck to his back. "You won't believe what Willow said last night when we took a walk in the Oakville city park."

Jack pricked his ears forward and whinnied.

"I knew I could count on you to listen. Now I really need your advice." Austin chuckled at his foolishness. "Willow told me she was falling for me. I told her I cared for her, too. A lot."

Jack munched on a piece of hay, as if content to merely listen.

"For a while we both had second thoughts about a relationship. What if she only likes me because I remind her of her dead husband?" He worked the comb over Jack's mane. "I can't be a replacement for him."

Jack lowered his head, his ears forward and relaxed.

"Don't sweat the small stuff?" Austin grinned.

"I get it, buddy, thanks."

Boots clacked and stomped at the entrance of the barn. "You talking to yourself, man?" Mac stepped toward Jack. "Or are you telling all your woes to Jack? He's a pretty good listener, I understand."

Austin swallowed the lump in his throat. He wasn't too comfortable knowing Mac had heard his conversation with his horse. "Naw. Just giving Jack a brushing. He was sick for a long time and deserves to be pampered."

Mac chuckled. "You ever need a listening ear, I'm available."

Austin set the curry comb in the grooming bag and turned to Mac. "There's a lot going on with our relationship."

"Yours and Jack's?" Mac roared.

Austin punched Mac's shoulder. "No, you bonehead. Willow. Her deceased husband is likely my twin brother. We're waiting for a DNA test and keeping it quiet for now."

"Whoa." Mac's expression changed from a smile to one of concern. "Sure, man. I'll keep it to myself. But that's crazy."

"Yeah, and what's more, the guy died of leukemia." Austin paced the floor of the horse barn. "I haven't mentioned this to anyone yet, not even Jack. But what if Willow and I married, and the same thing happened to me?"

Mac gripped Austin's shoulder. "Look, Austin. I

read an article online a few weeks ago. Leukemia isn't hereditary. Only five percent of cases have occurred among family members. Besides, we can't go around living in fear. God will take us when He's ready."

"Thanks, Mac. You're a true friend." Austin turned toward Jack and smiled. "And thank you, too, Jack. Good talk today."

~

Two hours later, Austin checked his watch. The horse barn mucked with fresh hay and water for all of the horses, he had a few hours before dinner.

He closed the door to the horse barn behind him and stepped out into the sunny afternoon. Since he'd considered the possibility that a map could be hidden in one of the outbuildings, might be wise to spend a little time looking around.

The sheep barn stood to his left and was partially empty since half of the flock grazed in the west pasture.

Austin walked past the vehicle storage shed toward the old barn. Was it his imagination that a shadow passed behind the barn and disappeared?

The chill of the musty barn soothed Austin's ears and cheeks offering relief from the sweltering summer heat. The familiar smell of hay, dust, manure, and aging wood filled his nostrils.

Wooden stalls lined the length of barn, divided

by an open corridor covered with hay. Daylight filtered in through the windows high up on the wall. The tall ceilings with the exposed beams allowed good ventilation.

Austin exhaled a slow, deep breath. In the cool barn, threats from intruders began to fade, and his nerves eased. He scanned each corner of the barn, attempting to think like Jeremiah would've in his day. Where might he have stashed a map?

Straight ahead, an old, rusty toolbox rested in the corner where the west and south walls met. It'd been there for as long as he could remember, a relic of forgotten tasks. Perhaps a long shot, but no harm in exploring every possibility.

He moved toward the toolbox, but the floor beneath him shifted. His foot caught, and he pitched forward, his forehead smashing against the post of the nearby pen—like hitting stone. He blinked through the shock and turned his gaze toward the spot where he'd tripped. A loose board jutted out, wedged at an odd angle.

A warm trickle rolled down his forehead, and he wiped his finger over the skin. Red. He pushed up to his feet and swayed a second. Better get to the house for some first aid.

Still feeling the sting of his stumble, he took a few cautious steps toward the door. Through the dusty barn window, he glanced out at the pasture beyond the barn and the bunkhouse. The trees and meadow lay quiet, undisturbed, and no one was in sight. A sense of unease crept down his spine. Had the board loosened over the past few weeks, or had someone intentionally unfastened it? Gripping the wooden stall, he braced himself, fighting off another wave of dizziness that threatened to pull him down.

He slowly trudged up to the main house, holding his head with one hand. A knot of anger built inside, accompanied by a lingering urgency. He got the message. The intruders meant business. He had to find that map before they escaped with Great Grandfather's wealth.

Chapter Twenty-Five

After lunch the next day, Austin set out to the horse barn to saddle up Jack. He brushed the bandage with his fingertips and caught his breath. Still hurt. Though Dad mostly frowned when Austin explained the incident in the sheep barn, Austin figured his father was more concerned than he wanted to admit.

Austin saddled Jack and rode to the section of the north pasture closer to the house. He ran his fingers over his pocket with the letter he'd received earlier today. The results of the DNA test. His heart pounded every time he thought about it. Emma was his biological mother, and that meant Jesse was his brother. When he told Mom and Dad at lunch, not only did his heart race, but his hands moistened. Yet no matter what biology said, Mom and Dad Ford would always be his parents.

The comforting bleats of the flock calmed his nerves. He guided Jack among the sheep, glancing at each for signs of health issues. Experience on the ranch had shown him that if one fell ill, the disease would quickly spread to the rest of the flock.

Something to his right caught his attention. A sheep lay on the ground. The creature attempted to rise, dragging one leg behind her. She gave a high-pitch, distressing bleat, and fell to the ground again.

Austin jumped off Jack and knelt by the sheep's side.

The ewe's leg was bent at an unnatural angle—an indication of a break. Bruising and swelling was visible around the area. No doubt the animal had injured her leg. Perhaps she fell on some rough terrain or stumbled on uneven ground. The responsibility for his flock weighed on him as heavy as one of his post hole diggers.

He checked his watch. What time did Willow get off on Fridays? He pulled out his phone and pressed her speed dial. "Willow, can you come to the ranch as soon as possible? I have a sheep with a broken leg." Nothing to do but get the ATV and haul the animal from the pasture to the barn. He whistled for Fred about thirty yards to the east wandering around the flock. "Fred, look out for this ewe while I go get the ATV."

~

Willow parked her van in front of the Ford ranch house and stepped out, wind whipping her hair to one side. She retrieved her medical case from the backseat. While she wasn't thrilled about Austin's issues with one of his flock, at least she had an opportunity to see him again.

Austin steered his ATV nearer the van as the clouds darkened the late afternoon sky. "We better take the ATV out to the pasture. The ewe can't get up."

Willow read the concern and compassion on his face. "Let's go." She jumped in to his vehicle and set her portable bag beside her feet.

The ATV bumped and jostled along the dirt road. Austin steered away from the path through a thicket of brush and high grass. "Thanks for coming. I considered trying to splint the leg myself, but figured you'd do a lot better job," Austin smiled.

She gripped a firm hand on his knee. "Don't worry. She'll be fine after we get her to the barn."

The ewe lay on the ground struggling to get up.

Willow slipped on her plastic gloves and bent down, gently touching the injured leg. "Let's get her to the barn. I'll disinfect the area then put a splint on that leg."

Austin's eyes and a furrowed brow showed his concern about the animal. He pulled a tarp from the back of the ATV. Together, they gently rolled the sheep onto the canvas and hoisted her into the vehicle. Returning to the sheep barn, Willow grabbed her equipment from her van.

The evening breeze picked up as the sun slid

behind the horizon. They settled the animal in a pen on the far wall.

"She needs fresh water and access to food—hay, corn, or other grain." Willow knelt down beside the creature. "I'm treating that bone now."

"Sure, be right back." Austin took off toward the entrance to the barn.

In the dim light, the animal's labored breaths filled the air, and Willow murmured soothing words, trying to ease its discomfort. After twenty minutes, the broken leg set, Willow gave the sheep pain medication and an antibiotic. "All right, you're going to rest here in this pen until your leg heals." She stoked the animal's head.

A sharp flash of light sliced through the sky, and thunder shook the barn, making the walls tremble. Willow tensed her shoulders.

The sheep jolted, and Willow's heart skipped a beat as the storm's intensity surged. She reached for the wooly creature, whispering a calming word to her. Willow's pulse raced from the shock of the storm's fury. She had to focus on the sheep's care, though the torrent's power raged just beyond the walls.

She stood up and quietly tiptoed toward the barn's front entrance where Austin had disappeared. As she peered out, she saw him approaching, now dressed in a raincoat, a sack of feed slung over his shoulder and a pail of water in hand.

Austin stepped inside, rain dripping down his

cheek as he moved toward her. "Are you okay?" Concern flickered in his eyes.

"Yeah, but I'm afraid our ewe was startled," she replied. "In any case, she's going to be fine. I have her leg set, and she's settled in her pen.

He put the pail and sack down near where the sheep rested. "I meant to mention this before I left to get the feed, but it slipped my mind. Last night, I noticed someone had been in the barn during the day. One of the floorboards had been loosened. I tripped over it and nearly went down."

Willow focused on the bandage he wore on his forehead. "I noticed the gauze but didn't get a chance to ask you about it."

"Yep, mom had to get out the first aid kit." He blew out a frustrated breath and ran a hand through his wet hair. "I'm glad you're all right. But I need to figure out what's going on here. And Willow, there's something else I have to tell you."

~

Austin led Willow to a hay bale at the entrance to the barn. "Let's sit here and talk." He couldn't put off telling her the truth about himself any longer. He sank down beside her.

Willow ran her fingers over his hand. "I see the tension in your face, Austin—and its more than a sick sheep."

Did she know him that well? Having been married to his twin brother, who shared many of Austin's mannerisms, perhaps she could read him just as easily. He grasped her hand and cradled it to his chest. "I got the results of the DNA test."

Catching her breath, she sat up straight and fixed her gaze on him.

Austin gripped her hand tighter. "I'm your husband's twin brother."

Willow clasped both hands to her mouth, eyes wide, and then nodded. "I've thought about this every day since we visited Emma. In reality, I'm not surprised."

"But the truth could be overwhelming." His gaze lingered on every detail of her face. "I hope this doesn't drive a wedge between us."

Willow brushed a tear from her cheek. "No one's to blame, but this is all so strange."

He exhaled a quick breath. "Yes, but we have to acknowledge the facts. I'm Emma's other son. Can we get past the truth?"

She paused, looking at something over his shoulder. "I miss Jesse, but he's with the Lord now." Her other hand gently traced his jawline. "Your face may look exactly like his, but you are your own person—unique in your own way." She pressed a soft kiss to his cheek. "I love how openly you share your thoughts, how you let me see who Austin Ford truly is." She took a steadying breath. "But can you accept that you've fallen in love with your brother's wife?"

Austin gulped. "This will all take time, but we have plenty of it—all the time the Lord has given us on this earth." He bowed his head. "Willow, will you pray with me?"

"There's nothing I'd rather do."

Austin bowed his head. "Dear Lord, only You have the wisdom to handle this matter. Willow and I have come to a new realization, but these are things You've known since the beginning of time. Please guide our steps, Lord. Protect us from those who seek to harm us and bring them to justice. And if it's Your will, help us discover whatever valuables my great-grandfather left behind. Amen."

Chapter Twenty-Six

Two weeks later, Willow gave Austin a high-five. "I couldn't have done this without you." She whirled around her clinic's examination room. The reality of the metal exam table, the cabinet with her microscope, supplies, syringes, and medications—well, she couldn't be happier.

Austin pinned the chart on the wall displaying the anatomy of the dog alongside the other two—the horse and the cat. "Your insurance company sure came through."

"And the Ford Ranch's generous donation." She smiled. "I'll open for business on Monday." She clapped her hands, her laughter echoing through the room.

Austin took a few steps closer to her. "Your clinic looks better than ever." He ran his fingers through his hair. "And it's been two weeks since we've had any disturbances on the ranch." He sighed. "Even though the sheriff hasn't caught the culprits at the ranch or your clinic, maybe we've finally seen the last of these troublemakers."

"I hope so." Willow arranged her stethoscope, otoscope, and thermometers in the drawer and glanced up at the security camera blinking green. "Your recommendation to install an alarm system was a great idea."

A knock on the door called her to the front office of the clinic. She smiled at the now familiar face. "Come in, Sheriff Banks. I'll be open soon."

The sheriff removed his hat and stepped into the office. "Everything looks great, Dr. Lawson. I've assigned an extra deputy to patrol your vet's office for as long as needed. Let's hope we don't see a repeat of this incident."

She brushed a strand of hair off her cheek. "Were you able to find out any more information about the intruders? I'd be interested in their motives. I still can't understand why someone would want to destroy a small-town vet's office."

"At this point, we don't have a motive. We'll continue our investigation until we find the perps. But if you'll remember, I mentioned we had a clue."

Willow straightened and clenched her jaw. "Yes."

"I have some new information. I suggested to my deputies we check security cameras in the area." He pointed toward the north wall. "The dry cleaners next door provided us with footage. Though the faces were blurred, we could see the images of two men entering through the back door around one a.m. that night."

Austin raised an eyebrow and shook his head. "Gotta be the ones who destroyed her equipment."

Willow grasped her throat. "So now at least we know that the culprits were men and that there were two of them."

"That's correct." The sheriff continued. "Since the fingerprints haven't provided any leads, we'll continue exploring other avenues. The incident happened over a month ago, so I'm inclined to believe the offenders have moved on to who knows where. Could be you won't have any more problems. Unfortunately, they may never be brought to justice."

"I suppose I need to face that possibility." Willow forced a smile. "Thank you, Sheriff. My next step is to let the community know that I'm open for business."

~

That afternoon, Austin tapped on the doorframe of Dad's office. The thought of Willow opening her clinic filled him with a sense of hope—hope that their peaceful community would remain free from further criminal activity from those two. "Got a minute?"

"Sure son. Come on in. I want to talk to you, too. I have to admit I couldn't run this ranch alone these days. In fact, I believe your mom and I are getting closer and closer to retirement. I hope you'll be able to take over when that time comes."

Austin held both palms up like stop signs. "Whoa. That's a lot to take in at once." He hadn't anticipated hearing those words from his father today, but they lifted his spirits. Knowing Dad trusted him with the entire ranch stirred up pride within, boosting his confidence.

He took a seat in front of Dad's desk. "Talking about your retirement has made me think. Do you think Tim would ever give up his medical practice in Lubbock and come back to the ranch?"

Dad scratched his neck. "It's a possibility, but only time will tell. Your brother is completely invested in his work as of now. In any case, I want you to take the reins of the ranch."

An inward smile warmed Austin's heart. "Another thought. I talked to the sheriff in town yesterday, and he believes that whoever ransacked Willow's office has left the area. Since we haven't seen any activity around the ranch, I wonder if our culprits have moved on as well."

"Could be." Dad rose and patted Austin's shoulder. "I appreciate you setting up the security fences around the north and west pastures, along with the cameras throughout the ranch."

"I've asked Mac to help me make daily inspections of the back pastures. Chet will pitch in when he's working." Austin exhaled a contented sigh. "I think we can put all of this behind us."

Dad returned to the desk and tapped a pen on his desk. "Do you plan to continue searching for the rumored treasure on the ranch?"

Austin folded his arms over his chest. "I think I've given up on that, too. Though Great Grandpa Jeremiah's journals mentioned a map he created, it could prove impossible to find given all the nooks and crannies around the ranch. Also, after all this time, it might have been destroyed.

"Your Grandfather Martin never found it, and I haven't either."

Austin hiked his leg over his knee. "I believe it'd be best for me to concentrate on my work here at the ranch, and if a map turns up someday, so be it. If not, it wasn't meant to be."

Dad gave him a thumbs up. "I'll respect whatever decision you make."

Austin's face warmed. "Speaking of decisions, what would you say about the possibility of a new daughter-in-law?"

A slow grin filled Dad's face. "I'd vote yes, especially if it's that pretty veterinarian."

"I'd like to talk to Mom as well, and maybe I'll get ready for a romantic picnic in a few days."

Chapter Twenty-Seven

Austin braked and parked the ATV under the giant oak next to Coyote Creek. The woman beside him, whether in scrubs or jeans or dressed for church, always made his heart pound. "Sit right there." He ran around to her side of the open-air vehicle and offered his hand, helping her out.

"Austin Ford, you're such a gentleman." Soft crinkles accented the edge of her eyes as a smile spanned her face. "Are we finally going to taste some of that food I've smelled since we left the ranch? Let me guess—fried chicken and apple pie?"

"My secret's out. And potato salad, carrot sticks, celery sticks, and bottles of lemonade."

"I didn't realize you were a chef."

Austin rubbed the back of his neck. "Well, I had a little help. I'm not much good when it comes to fried chicken."

The oak shaded a grassy space next to the

flowing water. He spread the blanket on the ground, opened the basket, and reached in his pocket. Yep. Her ring was still there. He hoped she'd always remember this summer day when he asked her to marry him.

Willow relaxed on the blanket and raised the lid off the wicker basket. "This looks delicious. I'm starved."

Indian paintbrush grew in clumps several yards downstream. He approached the flowers, picked a few, and arranged them into a bouquet.

Austin stood to retrieve the small velvet box from his pocket, his heart pounding as he prepared to kneel, presenting her with the flowers and a ring.

The sound of a sharp gasp made him spin around, his stomach dropping like a stone.

Willow's face was twisted in shock and pain as a man stood behind her.

The man with a dirty black Stetson and a long-handled mustache, one hand over her mouth and the other around her waist, dug his fingers into her skin, his voice a low, menacing snarl.

Blood rushed through Austin's head, preventing the man's growls from making sense.

Willow fought to wrench free, her other hand reaching back, clutching the blanket as if anchoring herself to safety.

Austin took a cautious step toward Willow and the man, poking the ring box back in his pocket as he breathed hard.

"Mmm, mmm." Willow squirmed and kicked, no doubt aiming for his legs and missing.

Austin ground his teeth at the realization, and a cold chill ran down his back. The man was the same person who applied for a job at the ranch.

Austin lowered his voice. "Let her go." He took a few more steps toward Willow.

Cold, hard steel jabbed into his back. "I wouldn't do that." A deep voice spoke in his ear. "You try anything funny, and I'll use this on you." The poke was harder this time.

Austin glanced over his shoulder.

The creep who barged into the community meeting at the pet shop rammed the handgun with even more force into Austin's back.

Willow squirmed again, but the first man held her tight.

A whirlwind spun inside, threatening to spiral out of control. "You came in here looking for a job. You said your name was Tex Brown, but I'm not inclined to believe that now."

"Well, I'll tell you my real name, but first you gotta tell me where the treasure is buried. That blamed map King gave us one time weren't no good, and we're sick of digging up that pasture north of your house."

"I have no idea what you're talking about." Cold sweat covered Austin's body. "I don't know the whereabouts of any treasure or even if the gold exists, and that's the truth. I've looked for it myself and have given up."

"Tex" scowled at the other man behind Austin. "Should we believe that? I've heard the rumor for years. There's buried treasure on this ranch, and I suspect there's a real map, not that fake one we got from our old buddy. That's why I wanted to get a job here. To look for clues and find the loot."

Austin itched to turn around and punch curly-hair in the face. But what would happen to Willow if he did? "My grandfather and father have lived here all their lives, and they've never found anything, so I'd suggest you give up. Look, let her go and be on your way. You don't want to spend the rest of your life in jail." What could he say to discourage this man from harming Willow?

The man tightened his grip on Willow.

The other one poked Austin's back harder. "What do you think, Billy?"

Billy growled. "We talked about not saying our names, Liam."

"Okay, okay." Liam snorted.

If Austin could keep the conversation going, he could buy more time and maybe get more information about the two. "One question. Who told you the rumors about the ranch, and what is your real name?"

"That's two questions." Billy gave a loud howl and gripped Willow harder. "You fool. Her dead husband's father, King Arnold, was my best friend. He came to Oakville after hearing about buried gold on the

Ford ranch. But he got a chick pregnant. The idea of being a father didn't appeal to him so he moved on. Later, he died in a bar fight."

Austin gulped. If the man had been Jesse's father, he was also Austin's father.

Willow's eyes widened as she continued to struggle.

"When King lay dying on the floor of that bar, I promised him I'd try to find the gold. What a break when we found out his son had married a woman named Willow and now, she was in good with you Fords. We're not dummies. She came to Oakville for the same reason we did—to find the treasure. And we're not jeopardizing our chances." Billy glared at Willow. "I deserve a piece of that gold, and I'm gonna get it."

Austin opened his mouth, but no sound came out, and part of his strength waned.

"One thing I don't get." Billy glared at Austin with steely, mean eyes. "A while back, King decided he wanted to make contact with his old girlfriend from Oakville. He heard she'd settled in a small town in California and went looking for her. But he changed his mind and decided he didn't want to catch up with her after all. He showed me a picture he took of her and her son. Here's the weird thing. You look exactly like the kid in the picture."

Billy didn't know that Emma had given birth to twins, and apparently neither had King. Austin's head spun with the new information. But he had to set Willow free before anything else.

Willow worked her mouth away from the man's hand. "Look, let me go and be on your way. It's like Austin told you, there is no gold."

Another thought sent a cold chill down his spine. "Oakville is a quiet town. You're the ones who raided Willow's clinic because you wanted to run her off. What makes you think she came to Oakville to find the gold?"

Billy gave Austin a scowl. "You moron. Why else would she come to this Podunk, one-horse town? She obviously knew about the gold. Her husband or mother-in-law no doubt told her about the rumors. We couldn't let her get the gold before us." He jerked her hard to keep her still.

Austin gave one more lurch to escape his captor. He freed himself and whirled around. The gunshot rang out, and a searing pain shot through his arm as fire tore through it. With the other hand, he knocked the gun out of Liam's fingers and kicked the weapon out of reach. Then he pulled out his handgun and pointed it toward Billy.

~

The sight of blood seeping from Austin's arm while holding a gun on Billy sent a storm of emotions through her. What was wrong with her? She knew self-defense. With all the strength she had, she spun around and drove a sharp jab into his eyes. Then she propelled her knee into his groin.

Billy groaned and dropped to the ground.

Willow dashed toward Liam's gun and grabbed it.

Austin, his handgun still trained on Billy, glanced up and cried. "Willow, behind you."

Liam lumbered toward her.

With all the nerve she could muster, she pulled the trigger, purposely shooting in the direction of Liam's leg and foot.

Liam howled and dropped to the ground again. "You're gonna pay. You're jest as mean as your husband's daddy."

With Liam still squirming on the grass, Willow reached for her phone. "I'm calling the sheriff. It's all over for you two."

~

Hours later at the ranch house, Austin switched positions on the couch and gently rubbed his sore left shoulder. "At least we can't blame anything on Mr. Whitlock." His snicker brought a stab of pain.

Mom hovered over him. "Honey, can I get you anything? Another pain pill or your antibiotics?"

Dad adjusted the pillow behind his back. "He just had his pills. The ER doctor said for him to take both meds on a specific schedule."

"Mom, don't worry so much." Austin leaned back into the pillow. "The doc said the gunshot wound was minor. I'll be feeling better in a few weeks."

Dad dropped down next to Austin. "Son, you've been through so much, and I couldn't be prouder of you. We finally know who was digging those holes on our land. The sheriff said those two will be locked up for a long time."

Austin glanced at Willow reclining in the chair across from him. "The real hero is that woman over there." He pointed to Willow with his right finger. "If it hadn't been for her knowledge of self-defense, I'm not sure what would've happened."

"That creep startled me for a moment. I'm sorry my training didn't kick in sooner." Willow shook her head. "Honestly, Austin, when I saw you in pain, I couldn't bear it. I asked the Lord for extra strength, and He gave it to me."

Mom walked toward Willow and patted her shoulder. "Our family is blessed to know you."

"Thank you, Mrs. Ford. I'm blessed to know all of you, as well."

Austin groaned, rubbing his shoulder again. "Willow and I learned some surprising facts today."

Willow nodded. "The men who intruded on the ranch were friends of Austin's biological father—King Arnold."

Austin shifted on the couch. "It's interesting that

King apparently never knew he had another son—me."

"Yes." Willow sat up straight. "What I've been able to piece together, King and Billy came to Oakville years ago when they heard tales of a treasure. While they were here, King fathered the twins and then both men left. Emma became desperate and fled to California, never realizing Austin had survived."

Mrs. Ford stared at Willow. "This is all so much to take in."

Austin's neck burned. "I praise Him that I don't have to live the ungodly life my biological father did."

Dad put his arm around Austin's shoulders. "Son, your rightful Father is the Lord, God Almighty, and you have no reason to be ashamed."

"I love you, Dad." Austin breathed in the sense of pride and validation.

Willow folded her arms around her waist. "We also found out that the perpetrators who destroyed my lab were Liam and Billy, the same two digging on your property."

Dad frowned. "Why would they want to harm your lab?"

"They thought I'd come to Oakville to search for the gold." Willow sighed. "They thought I might find the gold before they did since I'd become friends with Austin and perhaps had a map. They thought by destroying my lab, I'd get discouraged and leave town."

Mom gave her a sympathetic look. "They didn't realize God had a purpose for you here. He wanted you to remain in Oakville, and that was that."

"You got that right, Mom." Austin chuckled. "But as far as finding buried treasure—I'm done looking for hidden maps." He ran his hand over his pocket. The ring was still there. He'd have to find another time to ask her to marry him.

Chapter Twenty-Eight

Willow parked in front of the Ford ranch house. She stepped out of the car, captivated by the stunning pinks, whites, purples, and reds of the snapdragons that framed the flower gardens surrounding the home. Two weeks after the attack and she'd begun to breathe again. Knowing the assailants who ransacked her clinic and intruders at the Ford ranch were now housed behind bars in Dallas made her feel even better. The entire Ford family was more at ease, she knew for a fact.

"Come for dinner," Austin had said. "And park up by the house."

She took a few steps toward the expansive wraparound porch.

"Hey, Willow." Austin walked out and down the stairs. "Got something I wanna show you." A large grin filled his face. Did she merely imagine that his cheeks were rosy?

The tall rancher with light brown hair set her heart to pounding. Light whiskers dusted his cheeks, and his hypnotic green eyes captured hers. "We're going down to Jack's stall."

She furrowed her brow and looked toward the horse barn. "He's not sick again?"

Austin chuckled. "Nah. He has a surprise for you and wants to thank you for being such a great doc. But he wants me to put a blindfold on you as we go into the barn."

"What?" Willow giggled. "That's crazy. What does Jack have he doesn't want me to see?"

Austin smiled and slid his large hand around hers. When they arrived at the entrance to the horse barn, he pulled a bandana out of his pocket. "Okay, you have to put this on for a few minutes. We'll take it off when you get inside."

The cloth covered her eyes as Austin led her forward. The scent of hay mingled with dust wafted toward her.

Jack neighed in greeting.

"Good afternoon to you, too, Jack." She grinned.

"We can take your scarf off now." Austin ran his hands over the scarf's knot on the back of her head.

As the filmy material fell away from her eyes, she blinked and looked around the barn.

Twinkling lights hung from the rafters overhead. Roses and green ivy adorned the top of

Jack's stall.

Over the wooden fence of his stall, Jack bobbed his head up and down as if welcoming her.

Austin spoke behind her, and she turned to him. He grasped both of her hands in his. "The day we had the trouble with Liam and Billy, I'd planned a picnic—and something else, an important question I wanted to ask you. But we had to fight off bandits instead." He smiled as he shook his head. He held his hand out to the horse's stall. "Today, with Jack's help, I want to try again."

Willow caught her breath. Austin had planned to discuss their future, or perhaps …

"Jack is helping out today because this is where you and I first met—the day you came to the ranch to treat him for pneumonia. Unfortunately, you fainted that day. I'm hoping that won't happen today."

Willow clutched her throat as the realization of his intentions became clear.

"Jack has a question to ask you."

Willow smiled and turned to face Jack.

A brightly colored sign hung from Jack's neck.

She read the words. "Austin wants to know if you will marry him."

Willow gripped her chest, laughing until the sound faded away. Then, she looked back at the charming cowboy who'd stolen her heart.

He knelt in front of her with an open box in his hands. "Well, what do you say to Jack?"

How many times had Willow allowed herself to dream about what life with Austin Ford would be like? She'd married his twin brother. Could she love both men, and would she expect Austin to mirror Jesse Lawson? No. Austin was a separate, unique individual. Though she'd loved Jesse, cancer had separated them, and he'd left her to go to his heavenly home.

Austin's eyes grew wide, and he breathed hard. "Willow? Is anything wrong?"

She gazed into his gorgeous face. "I'd love to marry you, Austin Ford. You're God's blessing to me."

His shoulders eased, and a soft smile crept onto his lips. Austin slipped a beautiful marquee diamond on her left hand and stood. "You made me the happiest man this side of San Antonio. No, the happiest man ever." He twirled her around a few times before softly kissing her.

After they finally stepped back from the embrace, Willow lifted her left hand to gaze at her dazzling diamond. "Jack is a good helper." She raised her ring finger towards the horse and giggled. "Well, what do you think of my ring, Jack?"

Jack nodded and gave a soft whinny.

"I think he approves." Austin took her in his arms once more. "I love you, Dr. Lawson."

"I love you too, Austin Ford."

~

The following week on Saturday afternoon in the living room, Austin smiled at his mother. "I can't thank you and Dad enough for holding this engagement party." He squeezed Mom's hand. "I can't believe I'll be a married man in only a few months."

Mom kissed his cheek. "You couldn't have chosen a more beautiful woman. Dad and I are proud of you, son."

Austin chuckled. "I guess this means I'll never have to call the vet again when our animals get sick. She'll already be here. The Ford ranch will have its own resident veterinarian."

Mom smiled and patted Austin's shoulder. "I certainly do hope you and Willow plan to make your home here at the ranch."

Austin turned to join Willow out back. He'd never seen the ranch house look so festive. Fresh flowers filled every room, and the savory aroma of barbecue and baked beans wafted through the house.

On the deck outdoors, the tables were covered with blue and white tablecloths. Each one held a centerpiece of fresh roses and daisies.

The buffet table sat at one end of the patio. Erica and Mom brought serving dishes from the kitchen to the table. Jace, Charlotte, Peyton, Dad, and Mr. Langley took seats at the long, rectangular table with room for the entire family.

"All right, folks." Dad lifted his hand and everyone was seated. "I believe we're about to begin."

He lifted a glass of sparking apple juice into the air. "Here's to the bravest two people I know. Alone, the two of them fought off intruders, called the sheriff, and brought peace to the ranch once again." He laughed and nodded toward Willow. "Especially this young lady who whomped a six foot, mean ole cowboy all by herself."

Austin rubbed his shoulder. "Yeah, all the while I suffered a gunshot wound to my shoulder."

"Glad you're doing better, son." Dad lifted the glass again. "Here's to a long and happy marriage. And I hope I'll see some more grandbabies pretty soon, too."

Until now, Austin hadn't thought of having kids, but he supposed he'd enjoy being a dad one of these days. He stole a quick glance at Willow who grinned. "God willing, kids will be a part of our future. And another thing, I've given up looking for treasure because I've found the best treasure of all—Willow Lawson."

Dad lifted his glass again. "Yes, you have. I suppose giving up on the gold is a good decision. Through all these years, no one has found gold pieces. Perhaps it was a myth after all."

Austin nodded. "Yeah, merely a fairytale."

Chapter Twenty-Nine

Willow gathered a pile of silverware from the table, placed it in the plastic tub, and headed into the house.

Mrs. Ford smiled at her. "You are one of our honored guests." Austin's mother took the container from her. "You're excused from kitchen duty, dear."

Though her relationship with Austin was more complicated than most, marrying into this family was a blessing and the best decision she could make. She gazed at her stunning ring. Being engaged to Austin felt surreal.

Mr. Ford, cleaning the propane grill, waved at Austin. "Son, could you please return the ice chest to the tool shed?"

"Sure, Dad." He glanced at Willow. "I'm gonna take the ATV. That thing is heavy. Wanta go, too?"

Willow grabbed one end and helped Austin lift the container into the back of the vehicle. She took a breath of the fresh air tinged with damp soil, freshly cut grass, strawberries, and barbecued ribs. How different would life on a ranch be? She'd already experienced a glimpse when she began caring for ranch and farm animals. Her stomach fluttered with excitement.

They careened past the hayfeeder and the equipment shed to the tool shed which had to be the original building. Weathered slats made up the walls, and the window panes belonged to a bygone era.

Austin offloaded the cooler and rolled it into the shed. "This goes in front by the window. Dad forgets where he puts things, so when he comes in, he'll see it right away."

Willow glanced around at the room. Exposed logs formed the inside of the shed, and hardwood covered the floor.

A cedar beam, which had likely been used to reinforce a small portion of the back wall, lay at an angle. "Austin, look at this." Willow took a few steps closer. She wiggled the beam a few inches. The four-foot plank gave a squeak and dropped from her hand onto the floor. "Oh, I'm sorry. I'm not trying to tear your tool shed apart."

Austin walked closer. "This old building? No. It's been here since the Fords first owned this land." He leaned in closer to the wall and reached his hand into the gap left by the fallen board.

Willow laughed. "Careful. There might be critters that bite in there."

"Maybe." He ignored her warning, twisting his arm around before pulling his hand back out. "It's some kind of paper." He spread out the contents on the worktable. "Butcher paper treated with oil." And then he gasped. "Willow, it's the map. The map Great Grandpa Jeremiah left."

Willow moved in close behind him, peeking over his shoulder. "I can't believe it. What does it say?"

"It's a rough sketch of the ranch. See, here's the tool shed where we are now."

Willow pointed to the figure to the far right. "I believe this is the sheep barn."

Austin laughed. "I think that X on the rough sketch of the barn marks the spot."

"Yeah, but where exactly inside the building does the X point to?"

"The sheep barn is huge, and there's also a massive basement." Austin stared a little longer and placed his finger on some arrows pointing to the cellar. "This is where the grain cellar is located. We've used it for dry storage for as long as I can remember." He glanced at Willow. "This means that there is hidden gold on the ranch after all, and it's got to be somewhere down there."

Willow had never been in the barn's basement, but no doubt an enormous space would make exploring tricky. "Okay, but where?"

Austin pulled out his cell phone's flashlight and leaned closer. "It looks like the map is indicating a section of wall."

Willow grabbed Austin's shoulder as the idea hit her.

He widened his eyes. "What?"

"If this is where the gold pieces are hidden, do you realize the significance of it?"

Austin scratched his head. "Hmm." Then a smile covered his face. "Great Grandpa never hid the treasure in the ground as we had thought."

"And as Billy and Liam had guessed."

He grabbed her hand. "Hey, let's go to the sheep barn."

~

On their way to the barn, Austin glanced again at the old piece of butcher paper filled with Jeremiah's drawings. Were they actually going to find any treasure? Somehow, he doubted they would. If Jeremiah had hidden gold in the sheep barn basement all those years ago, then why hadn't any of his other family members found it?

Willow smoothed her hand on his arm. "Austin? Is something wrong?"

"I suppose I'm skeptical about finding treasure." He held the barn door open for her. "Only a couple of days ago, I'd given up on the idea. I'm not so sure about pursuing the treasure again."

"But, Austin, we found a map." Her smile

brought a sense of reason. "If it's not meant to be, we won't find anything. But you have to admit, it's worth searching for."

He turned to the lovely woman by his side, soon to be his wife. "That's why I love you. You're so practical and full of wisdom."

She shooed him with her palms. "We're wasting time."

Inside the sheep barn, Austin located the ground door to the cellar. "I remember Erica said she and Peyton hid down here during the tornado last year."

"How ironic if we do find treasure." Willow's eyes twinkled. "They were so close to it."

Austin helped Willow down the last rung of the ladder and breathed in the dusty aroma of onions and garlic. He headed toward the wall indicated by the map.

"Look at the shelf along that wall. I suppose Grandpa Jeremiah stored produce and jars of canned food his wife likely put up." She ran a finger along the shelf and stopped at a spot toward the end of the wall.

Austin's pulse raced as he looked over her shoulder. "What are you looking at?"

Directly above the shelf, one of the limestone bricks had begun to crumble.

"Do you have a pocketknife?" Willow's eyes widened.

Austin reached in his jeans and opened the blade. "Be careful. Don't cut yourself."

She laughed. "I've used surgical equipment

sharper than that." She ran the blade along the crumbling rock and swiped away the debris with an old bandana lying on the floor. She glanced back at the map again, reached her hand into the cavity, and then laughed.

Austin's mouth dropped open as he stared at the leather bag, cracked and worn. The brown had no doubt darkened over the years, and one seam had loosened.

Willow handed him the bag and continued moving her hand around in the small limestone cavity. "There's more." She pulled out two more bags and then wiggled her hand once more inside the spot. "That's all."

Austin stood frozen. He opened his mouth to speak but no words emerged. His heart pounded as the weight of the moment sank in. His great-grandfather's map had led to something real. The treasure had been hidden for over a century, and now, he and Willow had uncovered the family legacy. "Let's take the bags to the house. Mom and Dad need to see this."

He couldn't walk fast enough to the house. He set the three bags on the dining room table, knocked at Dad's office door, and walked in. "Dad, you've got to come see this."

Dad looked up from a pile of papers. "Can it wait? I'm in the middle of something."

Austin chuckled. "It's waited for three generations. I guess it could wait a little longer."

Dad leaned forward, tilting his head to the side

as he raised an eyebrow. "What are you talking about?"

"I think you'll want to come now."

His father pushed back from his desk and followed Austin into the dining room.

Mom stood by Willow, her mouth hanging wide open as she stared at the bags. She glanced up at Dad. "You're not going to believe this."

Austin placed his hand on the first bag. "This was a mutual effort. Willow found the map and pulled out the bags. I identified the location." He paused. "I'll tell you all that later. We need to look inside."

Mom gave her usual soft laugh. "Maybe there's fool's gold in there."

"We'll see." Austin slipped his hand inside the first bag.

Small, circular pieces of gold were nestled among the folds of ancient leather. He reached for one, and the cool piece lay heavily in palm. He rotated the coin. A warm luster caught the overhead light.

Austin's heart pounded hard as he stacked the pieces on the table. Each spoke of their age and value. His stomach leapt within.

Dad slowly shook his head. "Son, you've accomplished something that none of the other Fords have been able to do." He wrapped his arms around Austin's shoulders. "A hidden legacy belonging to the Ford family." Glistening moisture shimmered in Dad's eyes.

Mom squeezed Austin's hand. "I'm totally

amazed. I can't imagine how much these pieces are worth. You're a wealthy man."

Austin lifted his chin. "Mom, this find rightly belongs to all the Fords. I can't keep it for myself."

Mom swept a tear from her eye. "I love you, son. I suppose we'll need to call a family meeting soon to see what everyone wants to do with the gold."

Dad swiped a hand through his hair. "The most ironic thought has occurred to me."

Austin stared at Dad. Did his father object to sharing the gold?

"Friends of the man who fathered you had searched for the gold to steal it from you, but because of their actions, you searched for it and ended up inheriting it. No one but the Lord could've orchestrated that." He gave a soft chuckle.

Austin peered once more at the hoard of gold on the table. But the find could never be as important to him as his Lord, his family, and now his fiancé. The deep sense of connection wrapped around him. No matter the challenges he faced, he was never alone.

Chapter Thirty

Dr. Willow Ford raised her left ring finger, admiring the exquisite wedding band next to her stunning marquise diamond. Hers and Austin's backyard wedding had seemed like a dream. And then hosting the reception in the Ford's great room made the gorgeous October day even more delightful.

She glanced at her watch and then waved at Emma, reclining on the couch. Having her in attendance added a special blessing to the day. She giggled. Now she had two mothers-in-law.

Soon, she and Austin would leave for the hotel in San Antonio. A tingle raced her spine. Tomorrow they'd catch a plane for New Zealand.

The long glass windows spanning one wall offered a view of the elegant outdoor terrace which only a couple of hours ago held serving tables and folding chairs. Beyond the north pasture, the land stretched toward the base of the rolling hills. Willow's gaze drifted to the home under construction on the west side of Mom and Dad Ford's house. Hers and Austin's—with its open floor plan, expansive windows, and ample outdoor space.

Austin's warm presence engulfed her from behind, and she turned to face her husband. He wrapped his arms around her waist as she leaned into him. "Guys aren't supposed to get sentimental, but today is the best day of my life. I'll never forget our wedding day, Willow." He pulled her closer, his lips meeting hers in a tender kiss.

"Hey, you two." Erica smiled as she approached, a toddler on her hip. "Save some of that for later when you're at your hotel in San Antonio. You made a great choice picking New Zealand for your honeymoon."

"I agree." The thought of exploring the rolling hills, picturesque farms, and beautiful sheep farms took Willow's breath away.

Austin's smile spread wide across his face. "I plan to talk to some of the sheep ranchers for tips to bring back home."

Tim, followed by Jace, approached with cups of punch in hand. Tim, his tall, slender sibling pushed his glasses up on his nose and clapped Austin on the shoulder. "I'm happy for you, little brother." He glanced at Willow with a smile. "You've married a beautiful woman."

Jace poked Tim in the shoulder. "And she's a

top-notched vet, too."

Willow grinned. "You guys are too kind. I feel just as privileged to be a part of the Ford family."

Tim shook his head in amazement. "I can't believe it—you actually found Jeremiah's gold pieces, something no one else could ever uncover. Deciding to share the money equally with the entire family? That's incredibly generous of you."

Austin nodded. "Of course. We are all a part of this family." He snickered. "I doubt that any of us will ever hurt financially again."

Mr. and Mrs. Ford joined the group, each embracing Willow and Austin. Mom gave a warm smile. "We want you both to know how much of a blessing this day, and your marriage, is to us."

Willow dabbed the moisture from her eye. "Mom and Dad Ford, your acceptance of me into this family means the world to me."

Tim lifted his hand. "Since most of us are here, I need to say something before Austin and Willow leave." He paused, glancing at Mom Ford. "I'm giving serious thought to returning to the ranch."

Mom Ford's eyes widened. "You mean give up your practice in Lubbock?"

Tim gripped both of her hands in his. "Mom, I'm only thinking about it right now. I'm telling you now so you can pray for me."

Austin patted him on the back. "You've got my prayers, and Tim, I'd love for you to return to the hill country and live close to family again. Love you, brother."

Willow sighed a long breath. To think she had so many new family members now. But she'd never expected that family would include her deceased husband's identical twin brother.

~

Austin lifted his gorgeous wife over the threshold of their downtown San Antonio hotel. He whispered in her ear. "I love you, Willow, and pray God will always bless our marriage."

Inside the spacious, seventh floor suite, with a king bed and outside balcony, he gently set his bride down. He gripped her hand and led her out onto the balcony.

From the seventh floor, the downtown lights looked like a sea of stars twinkling and blinking. Neon lights flashed in reds, blues, and greens, reflecting off the pavement below. He gently kissed her forehead, a moment of quiet intimacy. "I know I look exactly like him, but I pray that you won't see me as my brother."

She trailed her lips along his jaw and smiled. "No need for any concern. I love you, Austin Ford. You're a godly man whom I'm grateful to call my husband."

A sense of gratitude overwhelmed Austin. This was their adventure together, a new chapter, a new beginning. He reached for her hand, intertwining their fingers, and pulled her close, savoring the warmth of her presence.

The End

Discussion questions:

1. Were you surprised at Willow's initial reaction when she saw Austin? How might you have reacted given the same circumstances?

2. What do you think motivates veterinarians to enter their field of treating animals' medical problems? How do you think a vet copes with the loss of a patient?

3. Describe the relationship between Emma and Willow.

4. What do you think went through Austin's mind as Willow asked him about his childhood?

5. How would you feel if you were in Willow's shoes when she discovered Jesse and Austin were brothers?

6. In the end, how did God bless Emma though she'd made a big mistake as a young girl? What does this say about God?

7. Name one reason why Emma was so grateful to Jesus. How had Jesus changed her life?

8. When "Tex" came to apply for a job, what was the name of the ranch he said he worked for? Did you notice a symbolic meaning there?

9. Evaluate the sheriff's investigative abilities. What could he have done differently?

10. Describe your emotions when you read Austin and Emma's scene at the time he discovered she was his biological mother.

11. Billy and Liam thought Willow had come to

Oakville to find gold. What was her real reason, and what does that say about her?

12. Explain in your own words Dad Ford's conclusion. "Friends of the man who fathered you had searched for the gold to steal it from you, but because of their actions, you searched for it and ended up inheriting it. No one but the Lord could've orchestrated that."

Dear Reader, if you enjoyed *The Hidden Legacy,* please leave a review on Amazon. In fact, I'd love to request a review for my birthday. Short and sweet would be great. You don't need to write an essay. Okay, it may not be November yet, but an early present would be fine. Just for that, you get a piece of my birthday cake.

Have you read book one in the Ford Family Ranch series? *The Novice Ranch Hand* is Erica and Peyton's story.

Peyton Langley must escape the pain of his past and finds refuge at the Ford's sheep ranch in the hill country of central Texas. Maybe among the springs, stony hills, and steep canyons he can forget the past. Only thing, he knows nothing about ranching.

Erica Ford helps run the Ford Family Ranch with her father and two brothers, but no matter how hard she tries, she can't convince the men in her family that she's as capable of handling the ranch as they are.

bit.ly/3YALxOc

An award-winning author, June Foster is a retired teacher with a BA in Education and a MA in counseling. June began writing Christian romance in 2010 as she and her husband traveled the US in their RV. Her adventures provide a rich source of information for her novels. She brags about visiting a location before it becomes the setting in her next book.

To date, June has written over thirty contemporary romance and romantic suspense novels and novellas. June uses her training in counseling and her Christian beliefs in creating characters who encounter real-life difficulties yet live victorious lives. She's published with Winged Publications.

June is active in her church and her ladies' fellowship group. She enjoys writing devotionals as well as fiction. She frequently attends writers' conferences such as Blue Lake Writers' Conference and Florida Christian Writers Conference.

Her novel, *The Inn at Cranberry Cove,* won the 2021 Selah award for Romantic Suspense. It is available on Amazon in paperback, hardback, and eBook format. In 2023, June won the Ames Award for her book *Christmas at Cranberry Cove*, book three in the same series.

Visit June at www.junefoster.com to see a complete list of her books.

Enjoy these books by June Foster

The Woodlyn Series
Flawless
Out of Control
All Things New

The Almond Tree Series
For All Eternity
Echoes From the Past
What God Knew
Almond Street Mission

Small Town Romance
Letting Go
Prescription for Romance
A Harvest of Blessings
The Long Way Home

The Cranberry Cove Series
The Inn at Cranberry Cove
Love Found at Cranberry Cove
Christmas at Cranberry Cove
A Home in Cranberry Cove
Danger In Cranberry Cove

Christmas Novellas
Christmas at Raccoon Creek
A Christmas Kiss

A Kiss Under the Mistletoe

Devotional
Dancing in a Field of Daisies

Short Stories
Someone to Call His Own
An Accidental Kiss

The Ford Family Ranch Series
The Novice Ranch Hand
The Hidden Legacy

Stand Alone Titles
Red and the Wolf
Misty Hollow
Lavender Fields Inn
Restoration of the Heart
A Home for Fritz
Dreams Deferred
An Unexpected Family
Ryan's Father
Eliza's Hope
The Other Side of the Fairy House
A Hometown Fourth of July